John G. Swindell

Rudimentary Treatise on Welldigging, Boring and Pumpwork

With Illustrations by John Geo. Swindell. Fourth Edition

John G. Swindell

Rudimentary Treatise on Welldigging, Boring and Pumpwork
With Illustrations by John Geo. Swindell. Fourth Edition

ISBN/EAN: 9783337390754

Printed in Europe, USA, Canada, Australia, Japan

Cover: Foto ©Andreas Hilbeck / pixelio.de

More available books at **www.hansebooks.com**

RUDIMENTARY TREATISE

ON

WELL-DIGGING, BORING,

AND

PUMP-WORK.

With Illustrations.

BY
JOHN GEO. SWINDELL, R.I.B.A. Associate.

FOURTH EDITION,
REVISED BY G. R. BURNELL, C.E.

LONDON:
JOHN WEALE, 59, HIGH HOLBORN.
1860.

PREFACE TO THE SECOND EDITION.

THE premature decease of Mr. J. G. Swindell, at the commencement of a promising career, has prevented the subsequent editions of his useful work from receiving the benefit of his care, or from recording the results of his more extended observations.

It was with considerable hesitation that I undertook to revise the work, because at all times it is a matter of delicacy to alter, or correct, the productions of a professional brother; it was especially so in this instance from the sad circumstance of Mr. Swindell's death. Moreover, on some points of detail, I did not entertain the same opinions as Mr. Swindell; on others the limits of our knowledge have been extended since his decease, by the researches of scientific men both at home and abroad, and by the results obtained in the numerous works executed in different parts of the country; so that forcedly this treatise is to a great extent altered from the one he left.

The objects I proposed to myself were precisely the same which Mr. Swindell stated to have guided him in writing the original Treatise; viz. to condense in a general practical manner many subjects connected with Well-work. As he said, "it would have been easy to enlarge upon any of them, but to have done so would necessarily have entailed a corresponding loss of matter in reference to the others. To avoid this on the one hand, and a mere superficial uninstructive glance on the other, has been the Author's aim. In furtherance of this object, the remarks on executed work, contained in the seventh Chapter, have been added. These precedents show, at a glance, methods of detail and arrangement which, if remarked on generally, would occupy much greater space; they also form a nucleus for observations which could only be brought forth by a long process of reasoning in any other manner : again, they serve to bind and connect together, by their very particularity, considerations which otherwise might pass unheeded, on account of their now apparent applicability." In the second edition a modification has been made in the descriptions of these works by suppressing some, and introducing others. It might have been objected to those originally inserted that they were nearly all confined to the practice of the neighbourhood of London, and it appeared therefore advisable to introduce in a work of such general circulation illustrations of the course followed and the results obtained under a greater variety of circumstances.

I have, in this edition, endeavoured to preserve as much as possible the text as it was left by Mr. Swindell, merely altering what appeared to me the faults of composition. The spirit I have endeavoured to retain, the letter only has been modified. The alterations are, however, extensive—and indulgence is craved for them on the score of the difficulty which always exists in a second party's placing himself in the same position and in viewing a subject from the same point of view as the person who has gone before him.

More copious information upon the subjects treated of in the following pages may be found in the communications of the Abbé Paramelle, M. d'Archiac, M. Hericaut de Thury, M. Garnier, and M. Emery, to the different scientific publications in France; in the more decidedly practical works of M. Degousée and A. Burat, from both of which we have borrowed largely. In the 'Traité des Irrigations' by Nadault de Buffon, much valuable information will be found with respect to shallow springs. In our own language we can hardly cite any other work than Mr. J. Prestwich's 'Treatise on the Water-bearing Strata of London;' but it is a host in itself, and contains proof of a skill, judgment, and careful observation which justify our regarding it as a model of practically applied science. From the detached papers by Mr. Clutterbuck and Mr. Dickinson, in the Reports by Messrs. Stephenson and Homersham, much valuable information may be obtained; as also occasionally from the Reports of the Superintending Inspectors of the Board of Health, although the inferences drawn by the latter are always to be received with caution.

The reader who would desire to study the physiological influence of potable waters—a branch of the investigation which has only of late attracted public attention in our own country—is referred to the writings of Hippocrates, who knew quite as much, if not more, of the subject than some of our modern authorities. In Thénard's Chemistry; in the Dictionnaire des Sciences Médicales; in Haller's Elementa Physiologiæ; in a 'Traité des Eaux Potables,' by M. J. F. Terme, of Lyons; in some communications to the Académie des Sciences by Messrs. Chossat, Dupasquier, Berthollet, l'Héritier, and Tissot; and in the communications of Dr. Angus Smith to the British Association, and in the Report of the last Commission named by Sir G. Grey to examine into the qualities of the London waters,—much valuable information will be found upon the subject. It is worthy of remark that the Report of the last-named Commission is directly in opposition to the doctrines which the Board of Health have sought to inculcate with respect to the qualities of water; and in this it is perfectly in accordance with all that has been stated by physiologists from the time of Hippocrates to the present day. All, or nearly all, authorities of any value agree in considering that waters holding the bicarbonate of lime in solution are the most wholesome. It appears also that the rule sought to be laid down that "the nearer the source the purer the spring" is very far from being of universal application, and that great danger is attached to the system of storing water in reservoirs. Such discussions are perhaps out of place in works like the present, but it is important that the public should be made aware that the Theories lately propounded are far from being received by scientific men.

The whole question of the physiological action of water is very ably treated in a 'Traité d'Hygiène Publique, par Michel Levy.'

GEO. R. BURNELL.

CONTENTS.

CHAPTER VIII.

APPENDIX.

WELLS AND WELL-DIGGING.

CHAPTER I.

PRELIMINARY OBSERVATIONS.

THE practice of obtaining water from wells is of great antiquity. In the Scriptures, the earliest authentic record of the human race, many instances are cited of the importance attached to them in the burning plains of Syria, where, from the accounts handed down to us, they appear to have been mere excavations in the sides of rocks and hills in which springs of water were plentiful, the water rising so near the surface as to be reached by a bucket attached to a short rope. In Greece, this plan for raising water was common, and in many cases the orifice of the well was finished by a cylindrical curb of marble, which was sometimes beautifully carved.

The method of boring for water is of an antiquity very nearly as great, although the precise epoch of its introduction is unknown. In Syria and Egypt, it is reported that many fountains fed by waters obtained in this manner exist, and that the greater number of the oases of the Libyan chain owe their existence to similar works. M. Degousée mentions that he delivered to the Pacha of Egypt a set of tools for the purpose of re-opening some of these wells, whose original construction probably dated some 4000 years back; and when the works were completed, it was found that the wells were lined with brick or wood. The details of the method used in sinking these wells are not known.

In China, however, the system of boring is ascertained to

A

have been long practised, and a French missionary, the Abbé Imbert, has given an account of the methods there adopted, which is (as M. Degousée rather dryly remarks) more characterized by credulity than by discernment. It is quoted in Degousée's 'Guide du Sondeur, ou Traité Théorique et Pratique des Sondages,' as follows:

"There exist in the province of Ou-Tong-Kiao many thousand wells, in a space of ten leagues long by five broad. Each well costs about one thousand and some hundred taëls (the taël is worth 6s. 3d.). These wells are from 1500 to 1800 feet deep, and of a diameter of from 5 to 6 inches.

"To bore them, they commence by placing in the earth a wooden tube of 3 to 4 inches diameter, surmounted by a stone edge pierced by an orifice of 5 to 6 inches. Then a trepan, weighing three or four hundred pounds, is allowed to play. A man mounted upon a scaffold depresses a lever which raises the trepan 2 feet high, and lets it fall by its own weight; the trepan is attached to the lever by a cord of ratan, to which a strip of wood is fixed; a man seated near the cord seizes this strip at each elevation of the lever, and gives it a half-turn, so that the trepan in falling may take a different direction. The workmen are changed every six hours, and the work goes on night and day. They are sometimes three years in boring these wells to the depth necessary to reach the springs they are intended to attain."

Almost all these wells give off considerable quantities of inflammable gas; there are some which yield, in fact, nothing else, and which are called 'fire wells.' It appears that the Chinese employ this gas as a combustible; doubtless it is nothing more than carburetted hydrogen, such as proceeds from coal mines in combustion. If M. Imbert may be believed, some of these wells are not less than 3000 feet in depth.

In modern Europe the art of well-making was long confined to the simple operation of sinking circular shafts, until land-springs were met with; at least in the greater number of states. In the province of the Artois, however, the use of the boring-tool appears to have been generally known and practised from very early periods. The most ancient well in France, whose date can be authenticated, is one at Lillers in the Artois, supposed to have been executed in 1126; and in that province, the facilities for this description of work are such, that a well is to be met with before the door of almost every peasant. In the north of Italy, at the very commencement of modern history, the arms of the town of Modena were two well-borers' augers; and a professor of medicine of that town published in 1691 a. treatise on Physics, in which many interesting notes are to be found upon the nature of different strata and water-courses, upon overflowing fountains, upon the manner of boring for these, and upon the excellence of the water they contain. Dominique Cassini, about the middle of the 17th century, endeavoured to introduce the system of boring more generally; and Belidor, in his work 'La Science de l'Ingénieur,' published in 1729, mentions the remarkable results which are often to be observed in these wells. He adds, evidently perceiving instinctively, so to speak, the theoretical conditions necessary to secure success in these operations,—"It were to be desired that many similar wells to those obtained by boring were formed in all kinds of places; but this does not appear probable, because certain circumstances in the disposition of the earth are necessary, which are not always to be met with."

In our own country, the first notice we find recorded of the application of boring is in the 'Parentalia,' in which Sir C. Wren is said to have adopted this precaution in order to ascertain the solidity of the foundation of St. Paul's in parts where the original surface of the ground had been disturbed. Subsequently, towards the latter end of the last century, many wells were formed by this means, especially in the Wolds near Louth, and in the London basin near Tottenham; and the real principles regulating the flow of water in these wells were ascertained, to a sufficient extent at least to allow of their execution being attempted with such probability of success as to justify their being commenced.

The execution of the Artesian well at Grenelle, near Paris, tended more than any other circumstance to direct public attention to this mode of obtaining water, not only on account of the remarkable success which crowned the efforts of the self-educated engineer, M. Mulot, in spite of all the difficulties and opposition he encountered in the long and anxious execution of the works, but also on account of the highly interesting discussions and the elaborate investigations to which it gave rise. MM. Arago and Walferdin followed the progress of the works in a spirit of enlightened philosophical inquiry which has led to the solution of many highly interesting laws of nature hitherto involved in mystery; and at the same time their confident predictions of the eventual success of the operation served to encourage M. Mulot, when too many others were disposed to throw doubt and ridicule on his efforts. The very remarkable confirmation of the *à priori* deductions of these philosophers affords also a remarkable illustration of the correctness of the received theory of the geological structure of the globe. But, singularly enough, the lessons afforded by this remarkable work have not been productive of all the scientific results we might have expected. Because water had been in this instance obtained in a position where there appeared no natural supply, it has been too frequently concluded that in all such cases the same results might be obtained, and that quantities of water were pent up in the ground, which only required to be tapped to allow of its rising to the surface. But there are considerations affecting the supply, and the overflow from the water-bearing stratum, which so far modify the question as to render long and patient investigation necessary before such expensive borings, as these deep wells usually prove to be, should be commenced. Many disappointments have thus been incurred in the search for what after all could not reasonably have been expected; nor would it be possible to cite a more striking illustration than to refer to what has occurred at Southampton. We shall have occasion to allude more in detail to this work hereafter, when treating of the present state of the science of Artesian wells.

The economy of the application of boring, instead of carrying down a shaft of considerable dimensions, must be evident. A remarkable instance occurred at Mr. Vulliamy's, Norland House, where, after having dug as for an ordinary well to the depth of 236 feet, a boring was commenced, and a copper pipe 5¼ inches diameter inserted. After boring 24 feet, the spring was tapped, and the water rose 243 feet in one hour and twenty minutes. The sand also blew into the well 90 feet, thus choking to a great extent the flow of water: by clearing some of this away, the water overflowed the surface at the rate of forty-six gallons per minute. This occurred in the year 1794. It is evident that, in this example, had the advantage of boring been fully appreciated, and the geological situation of the place been accurately determined, much needless expense in well-sinking would have been saved.

In addition to its use in operations of well-work, boring is of service in a variety of ways; for mining purposes, railway works, examination of ground, such as in the case of a doubtful situation, testing morasses, and other such works. The reasonableness of its application is self-evident; a few pounds spent in boring may save hundreds which would be expended if the operation were to be neglected. The accounts that are sometimes given of the quantities of ground swallowed up in filling a morass, so as to form a railway embankment, will occur to all as so much waste of material and labour. Generally, after a sufficient quantity of earth has disappeared to make the work assume a very serious character, a different method of proceeding is adopted. Now, by boring in the first instance, so as to ascertain the exact nature of the ground to be traversed, the right method of obviating the difficulty might be at once ascertained.

The application of boring to pile-driving has been attended

with great success in France, and with a considerable diminution of the expense attending the ordinary process; but it is
evident that it is only economically applicable when a certain
degree of difficulty exists in driving by the monkey in the
usual manner. In the 'Guide du Sondeur,' &c. before
quoted, is an account of the boring operations carried on
for fixing the posts of the electric telegraph from Paris to
Versailles : 476 of these were fixed in their places in the course
of a month; they averaged 3fr. 50c. each (2*s.* 11*d.*), some
being executed in hard rock. As the ground was undis-
turbed, no necessity existed for masonry to consolidate the
posts, which were let in to the depth of from 5 feet to 6 feet
6 inches. The passages for the tying-down bolts of the
bridge of La Roche Bernard were also formed by boring.
Indeed, the process is applicable either under water or on
dry land, either in a vertical, horizontal, or inclined direction;
and though its cheapness is most apparent when the hole is
comparatively small, yet it is sometimes practised of a diameter
of many feet, if the situation should not admit of excavation.
Such a case as the above is frequently to be met with in well-
work; thus in sinking iron cylinders through sand charged
with water, the water must either be pumped out, or the sand
bored through. The latter will always be chosen when the
rush of water is great, or when the pumping becomes expensive. To enumerate every case in which boring can be successfully applied would be useless; its capabilities for various
purposes, whether for wells, for draining, mining, building,
or purely scientific purposes, being now ascertained, every
engineer can judge of the circumstances which should dictate
its adoption.

There is, however, an application which is not sufficiently
known in England, notwithstanding that an account of it has
appeared in some of our professional journals; it is in the
formation of absorbing wells, by means of which the waste
waters of some branches of industry may be removed by
their being carried down to an absorbent substratum, and some

curious natural laws have been divulged by the experiments to which such works have given rise.

Thus, it has been proved that a well can absorb a quantity of water equal to what it yields. If, for instance, a boring yield 100 gallons per minute, and the water cease to ascend at 3 feet above the ground, by merely lengthening the tube 3 feet in addition above the permanent level of the water, 100 gallons may be continually poured in per minute without flowing over the orifice of the tube. If it be desired to make such a boring absorb say 500 gallons per minute, a pump able to raise that quantity is inserted in the well, and notice is taken of the depth to which it can lower the water-line. If we suppose it to be 15 feet, for instance, it will be sufficient to place a column of that length above the water-line, and the boring will absorb the quantity of 500 gallons. Should the water-line be below the surface of the ground, the absorption by this description of well may be indefinite.

Care must be taken to prevent any solid matters in suspension in the waters proposed to be absorbed from being carried into the boring, or they would rapidly choke it up. Precautions also require to be taken to prevent the contamination of neighbouring wells.

It appears upon a retrospective glance at the history of well-sinking, that its principles of execution are unchanged, but that the practice is by no means so; and that both as regards their mode of construction and materials, considerable modifications have been introduced. As the art is now practised, wells may be divided into two classes,—the common, and the Artesian wells. The former are dug, and necessarily of considerable diameter, through the strata near the surface, to the spring itself, and are supplied by the filtrations of the immediate locality; the latter (named after the province of the Artois, where, as we have seen, they have been resorted to for many ages) are not dug, but bored through such retentive upper strata as may overlie a permeable stratum, the outcrop of which is at a sufficient height to produce a hydrostatic pressure upon the springs sufficient to make them rise in the tube of the bore.

In carrying on boring and well work, a great deal of practical information applicable in other operations, and interesting in reference to the one going on, may be embodied by keeping a correct journal. The one here given is copied from a Model Journal by M. Degousée; and had such journals been always kept during the execution of the numerous wells lately sunk in the neighbourhood of London, by comparing them, much valuable geological information, and certain questions relative to the rise of water in wells, might have been ascertained with greater accuracy than hitherto. When a well is merely dug, of course the columns relating to boring-tools may be omitted, and when boring does take place, the list must be sufficiently extensive to embrace all the tools likely to be required. In the accompanying form the columns are filled up nearly at random, but sufficiently in detail to show how such a journal may be kept. Boring-rods have usually their lengths numbered on them, so that, if correctly screwed together in their proper order, the depth of the hole may be readily determined at all times.

JOURNAL OF BORING at   being

a search for

No. of sorts or samples of Ground.	1818. Days of Rest.	1818. Days of Work.	NATURE OF THE EARTH.	Chisel.	Auger.	Shell.	Spring Rymer.	Latch or recovering Tool.	Thickness bored at the end of each day.	Depth of Boring at the end of each day.	Thickness of each of the Strata.	Distance of Water in Well to surface of Earth.	OBSERVATIONS.
1	..	December 16th	Surface soil . . .	..	..	..	..	..	9 0	9 0	3 0	..	P.S. If possible, get level of surface above or under some fixed point well known.
2	..	..	Clayey soil . .	..	..	..	..	..	2 0	..	2 0		
3	..	..	Fine sand . .	..	..	..	..	..	..	..	..		Commencement of digging— [diameter.
	..	17th	Ditto . . .	..	8	6	..	..	9 6	9 6	8 6		Fixing guiding pipe for boring
	..	19th	Flint stones . .	8	..	6	..	..	4 6	13 6	..		Finish of digging.
	..	19th	Ditto . . .	6	..	7	..	..	2 0	15 6	8 6		
	..	20th	Ditto . . .	6	8	2	..	..	3 0	18 6	5 0		
4	..	..	Marl . . .	1	2	..	..	..	2 0	20 6	2 0		
5	21st	..	Marl . . .	2	2	..	..	..	..	..	..		Holiday.
6	..	22nd 23rd	Gray marl and calcareous lamina .	..	1	3	..	..	9 0	29 6	..		

CHAPTER II.

THEORY OF SPRINGS.

THERE are few branches of Natural History which have given rise to so much discussion as the theory of springs. The explanations which have been offered of the phenomena they present have been innumerable: some are partially true, and applicable in certain cases; some extremely absurd. It would be beyond the province of this work to relate the steps by which our knowledge upon this subject has assumed its present form, and it may therefore be sufficient to state that it is universally believed by the cosmogonists of the present day that the explanation of the flow of water from springs, whether deep-seated or superficial, is to be found in the fact that they are the lines of natural drainage; in other words, that they are supplied by the rain, hail, snow, and vapour precipitated upon the earth's surface, and part of which is absorbed thereby. A vast circulation of water is thus kept up. The rivers and streams, supplied by springs, in their turn contribute to supply the sea, which, together with the water generally, supplies the atmosphere by its evaporation, and thus completes the circuit. Though it has never been denied that land-springs, that is to say, springs found near the surface of the ground, are supplied by rain,—indeed, the fact speaks for itself, inasmuch as in dry weather they often cease to flow,—yet, that deep well-springs are supplied from the same source has been controverted; for, say the objectors, how is it that an increase of rain apparently makes no difference in the quantity of water, and, in like manner, drought appears not to affect them? A satisfactory answer to this will be found in the examination of the circumstances affecting such springs; it will be seen that they are generally derived from reservoirs of porous matter interposed between impermeable strata, which reservoirs will naturally overflow at the points where the permeable strata, supposing them to assume a basin-like form, touch the surface of the ground. The waters which overflow at these points form rivulets and streams, and the effect of great rain or drought will be only to add to or diminish the quantity discharged by these natural channels; whilst little difference will be found in the height of the water-line in the main reservoir itself. The word *little* is used advisedly, because it has been shown by careful experiments that a slight difference does generally exist according to the different seasons of the year.

A very important point to be ascertained in the discussion of this branch of our inquiry was, whether sufficient rain falls to supply the rivers and springs supposed to be so supplied. From the mean of a variety of experiments, it has been found that the annual depth of rain which falls in England and Wales is about 31 inches, supposing the same collected on the surface of the ground, allowing none to soak in, and none to evaporate. In like manner, the depth of dew has been found to be 5 inches. The whole may therefore be assumed as 36 inches. Of this quantity, part is disposed of in the supply of rivulets, springs, &c., and part is again raised directly into the atmosphere by evaporation. Assuming that two-thirds go in this manner, we have still 12 inches deep for the supply of the rivers and springs, a quantity as follows:— The surface of England and Wales being 49,450 sq. miles, we have 5280 ft. × 5280 ft. × 49,450 sq. m. = 1,378,586,880,000 square feet of surface; one foot in depth of water will change the above to cubic feet; so much for the supply. Now it has been calculated by Dr. Dalton that the Thames drains a tract of country of the area of 600 square miles, or about one-eighth of the area of the whole, so that if it be possible to calculate the water annually discharged into the sea by the Thames, a rough approximation to the total expenditure of water can be arrived at. By some philosophers, who have paid attention to the subject, it has been calculated that the river Thames discharges daily 13,000,000 tons of water, which, multiplied by 35·84, the number of cubic feet in a ton, = 465,920,000 cubic feet; this again multiplied by 365, = 170,060,800,000 cubic feet, the quantity annually discharged into the sea by the Thames alone: eight times that quantity, according to the above assumption, or 1,360,486,400,000 cubic feet, will therefore equal the total annual expenditure of the rivers of England, an amount not quite equal to the supply by the rain and dew, the difference in favour of the supply being 1,378,586,880,000 − 1,360,486,400,000 = 18,100,480,000 cubic feet. From what has been said, there can be no doubt that in this country the rain and dews alone are quite sufficient to account for the flowing of all the springs; and analogy would lead us to suppose that in all countries similar causes would occasion like results. Thus, on the shores of the Mediterranean, it has been found that the evaporation from the sea is sufficient to yield about five times the quantity brought down by the water-courses. Mariotte, and subsequently M. Dausse, have also ascertained that the annual quantity carried down by the Seine is not more than one-third of that supplied by the atmosphere to the district which it drains: the remaining two-thirds of the rain must then either pass off by evaporation or be absorbed by the vegetation, or serve to feed the under-ground springs.

The calculation of the yield of springs, when compared with the rain-fall of the district, will, in almost all cases, explain the origin of the former. The hasty conclusions to which unfortunately so many observers arrive, that the upper lands cannot yield the volume given forth by the springs, are only to be accounted for by the carelessness which so frequently marks this class of observations. For instance, in the singular documents lately issued by the Board of Health to explain the scheme for bringing water from the green-sand formations upon the south and south-west of London, it is broadly asserted that the streams those formations give rise to are greater than they could be if they were only fed by the rain-fall of the district. Now, the volumes carried down by these

streams were only ascertained by observations extending over
a few months of one year, and consequently were far from
giving a true average; and in addition to this, if the area of
the country supplying the streams had been calculated, and
the rain-fall taken into account, it would have been found that
the effective volume did not exceed on the average of the whole
year one-third of the quantity supplied by the atmosphere.

A partial examination of the strata of a district has led
some persons to imagine that springs cannot be fed by rain
falling on the earth's surface, because the latter, in the point
immediately above the springs, is separated from them by
clayey or rocky strata impervious to water. This objection
is of no weight, for it does not follow that because the
latter are supplied by absorption from the earth's surface,
therefore the rain must sink into it vertically, any more
than in the case of a common water-tank, where the water
is conducted by pipes from an exposed surface to a reservoir.
Now, if in the simile we substitute porous strata beneath
impervious ones for the pipes, and suppose that the former
are exposed to the rain at some distant points, an explanation of the whole matter is at once suggested. It will
be found that the existence of numerous springs may be
accounted for on this supposition, and that it also serves
to explain the difference between land-springs and those
called deep-seated.

When the surface of a particular district consists of a loose
permeable material lying upon a retentive substratum, the
waters soaking through from above will descend until they
meet with the obstacle it offers to their further descent. As
such waters are not under any hydrostatic pressure, they
cannot rise above the ground, and, on the contrary, they
rush into any artificial depression in the upholding bed: such
sources of water are called land-springs.

Deep-seated springs, on the contrary, are those fulfilling
more exactly the conditions we have supposed. Their supply
is derived from the rain-fall upon the surface of the porous

strata situated at a high level, passing under an impermeable stratum, which soaks through them until it meets with a retentive substratum; and then, if it cannot find, or make, an outlet, the water follows the lowest levels of the permeable strata, according to the laws which regulate its flow aboveground. If, under these circumstances, an opening be made through the overlying impermeable stratum, the water will rise to a height corresponding with the hydrostatical pressure upon it, excepting insomuch as it may be affected by the friction it meets with in its traject, or by the existence of any natural overflows. All Artesian wells are supplied by springs of this kind.

These general principles may be explained by reference to the figures 1 to 6. In fig. 1 a porous stratum is repre-

Fig. 1.

Porous.

Impermeable.

sented lying upon an impermeable stratum, and in this case a little reflection must show that the waters would collect at the lowest points of the depressions upon the top of the latter; and that if wells were sunk into this, the water from the upper stratum would flow into them. In fig. 2, if we

Fig. 2.

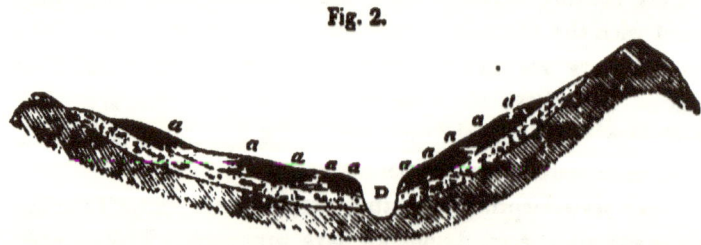

suppose the permeable stratum upon the sides of a hill to be

covered by an impermeable stratum *a a a*, and intersected by
a ravine or a water-course, it must be clear that the natural
tendency of the waters falling upon the outcrop of the permeable stratum would be to descend to the ravine, unless a
readier vent were offered at a higher point. In fig. 3, a portion of the waters would accumulate at c until they rose to a

Fig. 3.

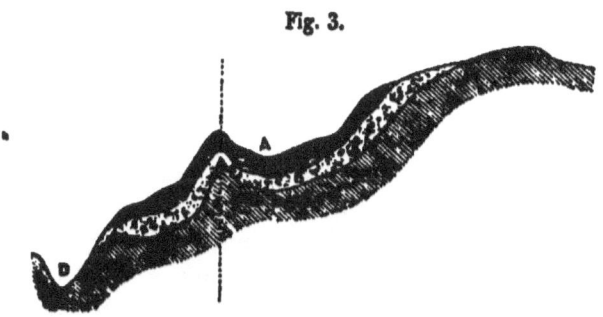

level above the projecting spur in the substratum; as soon
as they passed this, they would begin to flow over towards D,
and acting as in a syphon would effectually drain the intermediate porous stratum. In fig. 4 an illustration is given of

Fig. 4.

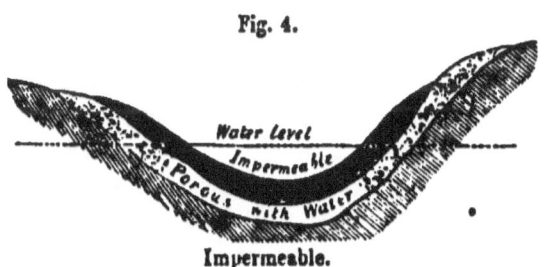

Impermeable.

the phenomena presented by the alternations of permeable
and impermeable strata in which no ravine or water-course
occurs to alter the normal conditions of the water-line. Fig. 5
is an illustration of the appearance often presented by the
chalk formation covered by the drift gravel; in this case the
bulk of the water would lodge in the depression below B.

Fig. 5.

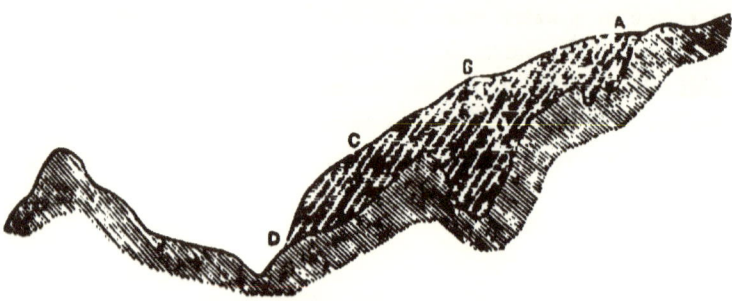

In fig. 6 is represented an ideal section of the London basin, showing the configuration of the strata, which serves to account for the supply of the numerous deep wells in the metropolis. All the water, falling upon the outcrop of the plastic clay and sand, passes under the impermeable blue clay, and if it be not afforded vent by wells sunk through the latter, it passes through the chalk, together with the waters falling upon the outcrop of the latter, until they meet the retentive strata of the chalk marl, or until they rise to the surface by any natural vent.

The assumption that all and every spring on the globe is derived from surface drainage alone, is perhaps more than is justifiable in the present state of science ; indeed some, by their brackish flavour, at once bespeak their direct oceanic origin. It is highly probable that some fresh-water springs do receive a supply from, and are modified by, the waters of the sea, derived thencefrom by capillary action. When the sea rests on porous matter, as chalk, no reason can be given why the water should not be absorbed by it, and affect to a certain extent the quantity and quality of drainage water which may be held in the same chalk reservoir ; and this more especially when the water-level of the springs is at or even below the level of the sea. It is natural to suppose this action would be felt to the greatest extent near the sea itself—a supposition borne out by facts. For instance, a well wall lately sunk at Newhaven, in the chalk, by the London, Brighton, and

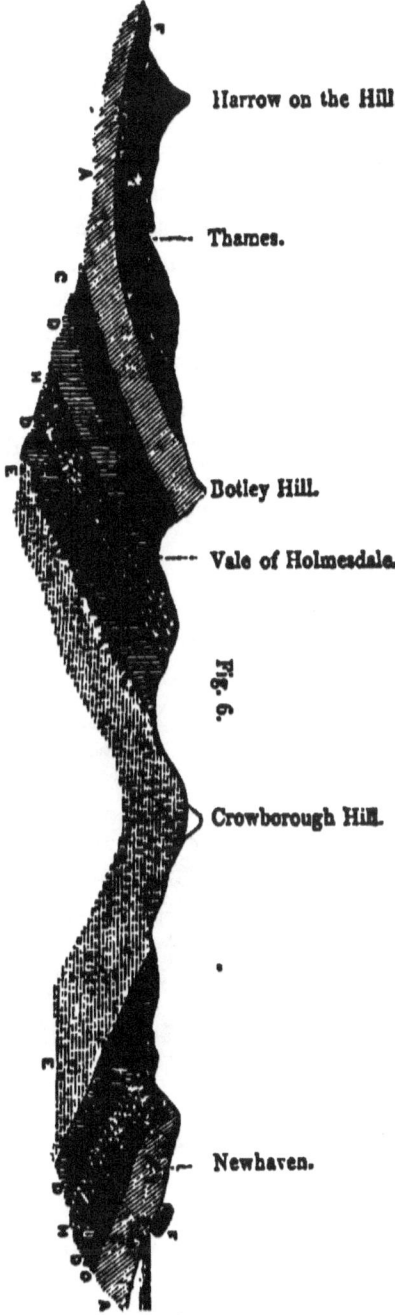

CROSS SECTION OF PART OF THE LONDON BASIN.—FROM F TO A, FIG. 7.

A Upper and Lower Chalk.
B London Clay.
C Chalk Marl and Fire-stone.
D Blue Marl.

E Iron-sand.
F Plastic Clay and Sand.
H Green-sand.

Harrow on the Hill.

Thames.

Botley Hill.

Vale of Holmesdale.

Fig. 6.

Crowborough Hill.

Newhaven.

The Sea.

South Coast Railway Company, yielded water which was seri-
ously affected by the percolation of the sea.   Reference to a
geological map will show that those same chalk hills, as well
as others abutting on the sea, are continued without inter-
ruption to the main chalk range on the western side of the
London basin; therefore, in a modified degree, the percolating
action of the sea water must be felt in all parts of the basin at
or near its level, and which are not cut off from this action
by any uplifting of the strata under the chalk, as in fig. 1.
Hitherto no disturbance of the strata has been observed
in this district which should lead us to suppose that any
elevation of the lower strata exists by means of which the
passage of the subterranean waters might be interfered with.
The lower portions of the chalk are extremely dense, almost
impervious, but not entirely, so that a possible though much

Fig. 7.

Line of Section of fig. 6.

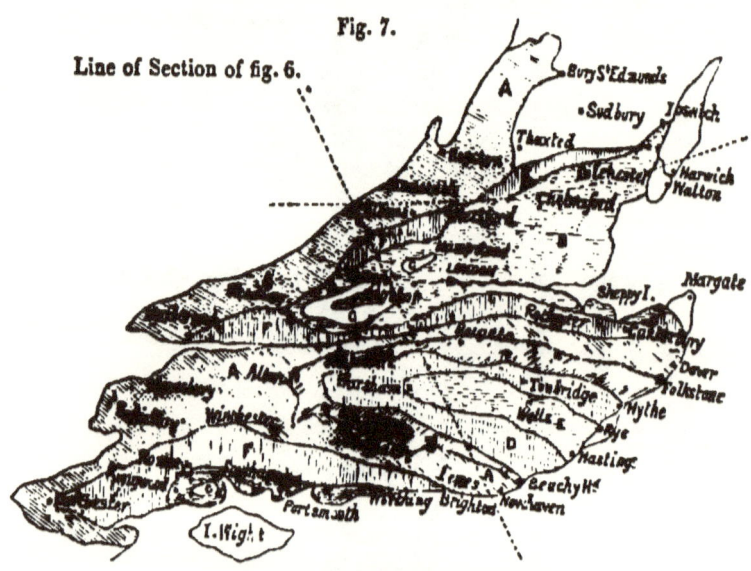

Geological Map of the South-eastern Chalk Range of England.

A Chalk.	D Weald Clay.
B London Clay.	E Iron Sand.
C Chalk Marl and	F Plastic Clay:
Green-sand.	G Bagshot Sands.

choked communication between the sea and springs derived from the rain being thus established, we may expect to find in this water, in a diluted state, such salts as the sea abounds in, due allowance being made for various decompositions which these salts must necessarily undergo during the progress of their filtration.

A reference to fig. 7, which is copied from part of Messrs. Conybeare and Phillips's geological map, shows the line of section represented in fig. 6, as also the direct communication, though not in a straight line, between the chalk of Newhaven and the range on the western and north-western side of the basin.

But although some springs found near the sea-shore are unquestionably affected by infiltration from the latter, the theory that those occurring inland are supplied by rain, hail, dew, snow, &c., which originally are raised into the atmosphere by evaporation, is now allowed to be correct by all whose opinions are of any value. That until comparatively within a few years the discussion should have been unsettled, is not to be wondered at. Until Geology showed, by explaining the nature of the crust of the earth, the natural channel for subterranean currents, and accurate experiments had determined the immense extent of natural though unseen and unfelt evaporation, no decisive proof could be given to settle and determine the question. Science has, however, now so far advanced that we can recognize the cause and the means whereby the alternate exhaustion and replenishment of the subterranean reservoirs are accomplished.

Before illustrating more particularly the various circumstances affecting the supply of water to springs, some of the most remarkable may be mentioned; and among them, the hot springs of Iceland claim attention. One of these, called the Great Geyser, is thus described:—The fountain is situated in a circular mound of matter, deposited by the water itself during the lapse of ages. In the centre of this basin a perpendicular inlet, about 10 feet diameter, descends into the earth, and communicates with the supply. The basin is usually covered, to a depth of about 4 feet, with clear hot water, which flows away by two passages situated in the sides of the basin. At the time of eruption, which occurs at intervals, the first signal is a rumbling noise and low report; after which a few jets of water are thrown up; the jets become higher, and the noise becomes louder, till at last a defined jet, 50 to 100 feet high, is formed, and of a diameter equal to the main inlet: the eruptions seldom last longer than a few minutes, and they occur at irregular intervals, seldom exceeding many hours. The water has the property of incrusting with mineral·matter objects over which it flows, also covering the parts round about it with silicious incrustations.

The fountains of Vaucluse and Nimes are equally remarkable on account of their volume. The former, directly after leaving the ground, is known as the river Sorgue, and is of such immense volume as to yield 444 tons of water per minute in the driest seasons, and 1330 tons in very wet weather. The latter is of smaller volume, but interesting on account of its intimate connection with the rain-fall; thus, in dry weather, it hardly yields more than one ton and a half per minute; if, however, any rain fall on the north-west of the town, even at a distance of four or five miles, the volume almost instantly increases to ten tons. The river Loiret is also supplied in precisely the same manner as the Sorgue: it rises in a large basin with considerable force, and flows away a river navigable for barges of two or three hundred tons burden.

Spallanzani mentions a spring of fresh water rising in the sea in the Gulf of Spezzia at a distance of sixty yards from the shore. It forms a dome upon the surface of the sea about 30 yards diameter, with an elevation of about 16 inches in the centre, and is composed of a number of vertical jets, which are very perceptible when the sea is calm. Many other such sources of fresh water have been recorded; for instance, in the Bay of Xagna, off the Cape San Martino, in the principality of Monaco, and in the Indian Ocean, about 100 miles from the shore.

The account of the two following springs is copied into Rees's Cyclopædia from the Philosophical Transactions:

"In the diocese of Paderborn, Westphalia, there is a spring which disappears twice in twenty-four hours, and always returns at the end of six hours, with a great noise, and with so much force as to turn three mills not far from its source. It is called the Bolder Horn, or Boisterous Spring." Again, "At Broseley, near Wenlock, in Shropshire, there is a famous boiling well, which was discovered in June, 1711, by an uncommon noise in the night, so great that it awakened several people, who, being desirous to find what it was owing to, at length found a boggy place under a little hill, not far from the Severn, and perceiving a great shaking of the earth and a little boiling up of the water through the grass, they took a spade, and digging up some part of the earth, the water flew to a great height, and was set on fire by a candle. This water was for some time afterwards constantly found to take fire, and burn like spirit of wine; and after it was set on fire, it would boil the water in a vessel sooner than any artificial fire, and yet the spring itself was as cold as any whatever. This well was lost for many years, and not recovered till May, 1746, when, by a rumbling noise under-ground like to that the former well made, it was hit upon again, though in a lower situation and thirty yards nearer the river: the well is four or five feet deep, and six or seven wide; within that is another less hole of like depth, dug in the clay, at the bottom of which is placed a cylindric earthen vessel of four or five inches diameter at the mouth, having the bottom taken off, and the sides well fixed in the clay rammed close about it. Within the pot is a brown water, thick as puddle, continually forced up by a violent motion, beyond that of boiling water, and a rumbling hollow noise, rising and falling by fits five or six inches; it may be fired by a candle at a quarter of a yard distance, and it darts and flashes in a violent manner about half a yard high; it has been left burning forty-eight hours without any sensible diminution."

It is needless to remark that the above phenomenon is owing merely to the presence of a portion of gas brought to the surface in combination with the water.

CHAPTER III.

RULES FOR FINDING SPRINGS, AND LAWS OF SUBTERRANEAN WATERS.

FOR ages many absurd fables were believed with respect to the best methods of discovering springs, and even at present the divining-rod has not lost its partisans. These fables owed their origin not only to the credulity of the public, but to the quackery of those professing the art. If, however, we pass over these prejudices, there are some indications which may lead to the discovery of springs in cases where nothing would appear, to those unaccustomed to observations of natural phenomena, to induce a belief in their existence. The following are some of the most simple:

In the early part of the year, if the grass assume a brighter colour in one particular part of a field than in the remainder, or, when the latter is ploughed, if a part be darker than the rest, it may be suspected that water will be found beneath it.

In summer, the gnats hover in a column, and remain always at a certain height above the ground, over the spots where springs are concealed.

In all seasons of the year, more dense vapours arise from those portions of the surface from which, owing to the existence of subterranean springs, a greater degree of humidity gives rise to more copious exhalations, especially in the morning or the evening. It is for this reason that the well-sinkers of Northern Italy go in the morning to the places near which it is desired to sink a well; they lie down upon the ground, and look towards the sun to endeavour to discover the places in the neighbourhood from which denser vapours may arise than from the rest of the field.

The springs to which these rules apply are such only as are near the surface; when the source is lower, they are rarely sufficient, and the only safe guide is a boring; but to execute such operations with any chance of success, a certain knowledge of elementary Geology is absolutely necessary.

Provided that the sources do not descend to any very great depth, the principle *that subterranean waters follow precisely similar laws to those upon the surface* holds good; but when they are very deep-seated, many disturbing causes, to be noticed hereafter, modify their action. If, in a valley formed in a diluvial or alluvial deposit lying upon a more retentive stratum, the two sides are of the same height, the water must be sought in the middle; and if, on the contrary, one side be steeper than the other, the stream would pass near the steeper side; in both cases supposing that the materials of the upper stratum are equally permeable throughout, and that the depression of the lower stratum presents a tolerably regular basin-like depression. Springs are not often to be met with at the head of valleys, but they are much more frequently to be found at the intersection of the secondary valleys with the principal one; and the most favourable point for finding water is usually that which is the furthest from the intersection of these valleys, and in the lower parts of the plain succeeding them, at precisely those positions where there is the least water upon the surface.

When the transverse valleys, giving forth streams to a river in the bottom of a longitudinal valley, are nearly at right angles to the direction of the latter, the quantity of water they yield is much less than when they form an angle with it. This law holds good equally with subterranean and with surface waters, and it may therefore be laid down as a maxim that the most favourable point for seeking a supply by a well would be at the mouth of long transverse valleys inclined to the principal one.

When, as we have before supposed, and as in fact occurs in
the London basin, permeable strata are exposed over a great
surface of country, and pass under more retentive ones, whilst
at the same time they themselves lie upon others of that
nature, by the usual laws of hydrodynamics the water falling
upon their outcrop will descend to the lowest level of the basin,
nor will it begin to overflow until the whole of the depressed
portion is saturated. A boring through the upper stratum
will then become filled by the water from below to a point
corresponding with the altitude at which the waters are maintained in the basin by the natural overflows. These abstract
principles, however, are only applicable when the basin is not
disturbed; and it is particularly to be noticed that the existence of any large fissure in the external ridge of the basin,
giving passage to a water-course, will be found to regulate
the height of the waters to a very considerable distance from it
on either side. If, however, any extensive fault exist in the
bottom of the basin, by means of which the permeable stratum
should be placed in communication with any other of a similar
character, the waters will necessarily flow into the latter. The
success of a boring for an Artesian well depends, in fact, so far
as the mere retention of the waters is concerned, upon the perfection of the basin formed by the upholding stratum; and, so
far as the height of the water-line is concerned, upon the level
of the streams flowing from the water-bearing stratum.

The existence of causes susceptible of modifying to so great
an extent the success of an operation of this kind is not sufficiently known, either to the public in general, or to those who
by their professional position ought to be better informed.
Unfortunately, the *science* of well-boring does not exist in
England, and the execution of this description of work is
usually left to mere practical men. The consequence has been,
that several wells have been commenced, have given rise to
great outlay, and, after disappointing the hopes of all concerned, have been abandoned. It is true that the knowledge
of the geological disturbances of strata, often hidden entirely,

must be always to a great extent hypothetical, but there are indications sufficiently clear to lead any practised Geologist to say beforehand whether any disturbance or fault exist likely to compromise the work proposed to be executed. With the most elaborate investigation and the most extensive knowledge, there is always a degree of chance about the first well bored for the purpose of reaching deep springs in any district. It is not therefore surprising that the majority of the attempts hitherto made in our country should have been failures.

The remarkable success of the Artesian well of Grenelle appears to have inspired a fever for undertaking others of a similar nature; and it is even now almost universally considered that if a boring be carried through the chalk into the green-sand, the water will rise above the ground. But in the first place it is to be observed that in the Paris basin the supply for the wells of Elbœuf and of Grenelle is derived from the lower green-sand which lies upon the retentive strata of the Wealden, and that it enters the sand at a point very much above the position of the wells, as also that the last considerable streams from the green-sand are at a much higher level than the same position. Similar borings near Calais have signally failed; for the subcretaceous formations there repose upon the carboniferous strata, without the interposition of the oolites, the lias, or any of the intermediate series. In this case the only chance of success would have been in finding some depression in the older formations filled with water, but of course it could never rise to any useful height.

The well at Southampton has afforded also some very important lessons with respect to the disturbances or modifications likely to be met with in the prosecution of such works. It was commenced at a point about a mile and a half from the sea, and 140 feet above the level of the high tides. As too frequently happens, no survey of the entering ground of the green-sand formations was made before commencing it; nor were the disturbances of the chalk strata, the only ones exposed in a manner able to furnish any valuable indications,

taken into account. Now it happens that the green-sand ridge
is disrupted in several places on the edge of the basin supposed
to hold the waters from which the well was expected to be
supplied, and important rivers flow away from it at those
places, at levels little above the ground at the well.   Should a
water-bearing stratum exist, therefore, the water can rise very
little above the ground, even supposing that all the other
necessary conditions be fulfilled.   But the whole of this part
of the country has been disturbed in a very remarkable manner.   A very strongly marked fault exists in the chalk near
Winchester, and continues to the sea-shore near Portsmouth.
The sea has formed two large breaches in the containing basin
of the green-sand on the east and west of the Isle of Wight.
At the back of the island the marks of geological disturbance
are even more evident than upon the north of Southampton ;
the strata are contorted, and even tilted up in a vertical
direction.   The same facts occur also more to the south-west,
near the Isle of Purbeck, so that there appears little reason to
believe that the basin is continuous; and at any rate the sea is
in direct communication with the green-sand formations: if,
therefore, it do not affect the quality of the water contained in
the green-sand, it must regulate the water-line, and cause it to
take a regular inclination corresponding nearly with a line
drawn from the last great inland overflow to the sea water-
level.   But it is found that the water obtained from the chalk
itself in the present state of the work is strongly affected by
the infiltration through the body of the rock from the sea.   If
this be the case with a substance comparatively so dense as
the chalk, the probability that the same effect will take place
with the more pervious materials of the subcretaceous rocks
amounts almost to a certainty.

Again, in all cases where wells have been sunk to a great
distance from the surface, it is known that at a certain point
the temperature becomes constant, and that beyond this it
increases according to a law susceptible of modification by
local circumstances.   Mr. Paterson (Edin. New Phil. Mag.

1839) gives the mean rate of increase in Scotland as being about 1° Fahrenheit for about 48 feet of descent. M. Walferdin found in Paris the increase was at the rate of 1·8 Fahrenheit for every 102 feet 10½ inches (or 1 centigrade for 30^m·87). M. de Girardin found at Rouen that it was about 1·8 for 67 feet 4 inches in one case and 1·8 for 100 feet descent in another; whilst the more accurate experiments upon the Artesian well of Grenelle show that the increase there is with remarkable regularity 1·8 Fahrenheit for 106 feet descent below the point of constant temperature, which is about 93 feet 6 inches from the surface of the ground at the Observatory of Paris, and marks a little more than 53° Fahrenheit. This would give an increase of temperature of about 1° Fahrenheit to 59 feet descent. This important law does not appear to have been much attended to in England, or certainly, as in the case of Southampton, the notion of obtaining the whole supply of the town from a deep-seated Artesian well would never have been entertained. The boring has been carried to a depth of 1320 feet nearly, still in the chalk, so that even did a supply of soft water exist at that depth, it would have a temperature of nearly 75° Fahrenheit; and as in all probability it would be necessary to descend 250 feet deeper before a copious supply could be obtained, the water from that depth would be about 80° Fahrenheit. From these combined reasons, the town of Southampton have been induced to abandon the boring on their Common,—unfortunately not before they had spent a very large sum of money upon a work which, if a survey of the district had been made by a competent person, would never have been commenced.

The secondary rocks frequently give off powerful springs without any apparent indication of the existence of the interchange of strata we have hitherto considered. Well-known instances of this occur in the springs from the chalk near the head of the New River, at Chadwell and Amwell, at Otterbourne, near Southampton, and at several other points in the valleys of the great chalk mass of the south-west of England. It will, however, always be found that these springs occur in valleys much below the general level of the formation, and their overflow usually corresponds with the existence of some fissure above a harder and more retentive bed than the mass of the chalk. The same remark holds good with the oolites and the lias; but, in addition to the inequality of texture in the bulk of the formation, these particular ones are more likely to throw off springs, owing to the existence of numerous intercalated beds of stiff clay. It rarely happens, however, that these retentive strata can be traced with certainty over a sufficient area to warrant the commencement of any expensive works upon them.

The primary rocks are even more unfavourable than the older secondary rocks for the ascertaining by any abstract rules the existence of springs. Their stratification is rarely persistent over a great extent of country, and the permeable materials, forming as it were filters, so seldom exist, as to make the occurrence of deep-seated springs very rare. Water may permeate these rocks in 'their numerous fissures, but necessarily it is impossible to predicate what may be their direction, or what conditions of hydrostatical pressure may exist. It may be asserted, indeed, that no abstract law prevails regulating the flow of water in these strata, and consequently that no boring should be attempted in them until the last extremity, because its success must be a mere matter of chance. For further details upon this subject consult Chapter VIII.

If many Artesian wells be sunk in the same stratum and be supplied by the same deep-seated springs, it becomes necessary to ascertain the rate of inclination of the waterline before any exact conclusions can be arrived at with respect to the definite results of a new boring. Of course, as the outcrop of the water-bearing stratum is only exposed over a certain area, the quantity it can yield must be limited; and for the same reason, if much water be withdrawn at a high level, the lower wells must suffer. That this is a real danger is proved by the state of the wells near London, supplied by the water filtering through the plastic clay. So many have been sunk, that very few of those which formerly overflowed the surface now rise to within some distance of it, and the volume yielded is also considerably reduced. The wells in the chalk near London are also producing the same result, and the water-line is annually lowering. The Rev. J. C. Clutterbuck, of Watford, who has paid great attention to this subject, has found that the water-line of the chalk near London has a general inclination of 13 feet in a mile upon a line drawn from Watford to the Thames, until we approach Kilburn, where a depression takes place, owing to the pumping around London, as he supposes. North of Watford, the rate of inclination was found to be as much as 200 feet in fourteen miles, but it was affected by the degree of saturation of the lower strata. In the Hampshire chalk basin, the rate of inclination has been stated to be 13 feet in a mile; so that numerous local circumstances require to be taken into account before any decided opinion can be arrived at upon this point, and equally numerous observations are requisite to furnish the elements of any philosophical reasoning upon the subject: in the last-named geological basin, however, it is more easy to observe the phenomena attending the inclination of the water-line, because no pumping takes place at the lower end to interfere with its normal condition. We find that from the well at East Oakley (about sixteen miles from Southampton) the water-level, which is there about 302 feet above the Ordnance datum, lowers to about 100 feet at the well upon the Southampton Common. But the rate at which the water-line lowers is far from being regular; it is more rapid near the summit, more gradual as we approach the sea, and may be represented by a parabolic curve. There are local irregularities occasioned by the outburst of considerable springs, due probably to some dislocation of the strata; but the general inclination prevails with tolerable regularity.

Stated generally, the laws regulating the height to which water will rise in an Artesian well are as follows: it will rise to the height of the point of supply, with a diminution caused —1st, by the loss of some portion of the water through fissures; 2ndly, by the friction it meets with in traversing the water-bearing stratum; but it must always be borne in mind that the existence of a large natural overflow will lower the general water-line to its own level.

The phenomena of intermittent springs may be explained upon the principle that under-ground waters follow the same law as those flowing upon the surface: if a natural syphon be supposed to communicate with some subterranean basin, and it discharge the water more rapidly than the supply arrive, the reservoir will from time to time be so lowered that the syphon will cease to act. Under these circumstances the flow will be interrupted until the water rises again in the syphon to a height sufficient to cause a recommencement of its action. This alternation of flow will happen at intervals corresponding with the proportion between the capacity of the supply and of the discharging syphon. And finally, we may state that no apparent anomalies exist which may not be explained by the geological and hydrodynamical considerations above detailed.

CHAPTER IV.

PRACTICE OF WELL-DIGGING.

THE practice of well-digging may be properly classed under two divisions, digging or excavating being one, and steining or lining with brickwork or stone the other; in the case of hard chalk or rock, the latter operation is dispensed with, the work being confined solely to excavating,— a lining of brickwork being quite unnecessary for the stability of the work. Wells are usually of a circular form, and those which are merely

picked in the solid strata lack the regularity of the nearly
perfect cylinder of brickwork : such wells, however, generally
require steining to some depth from the surface of the ground,
owing to the looseness of the surface soil ; this is exemplified
in many parts of Hertfordshire and elsewhere, where a gravelly
surface soil overlies the chalk.   The mere excavation of a well
requires but little skill, though at times it is a matter of
great labour, requiring in hard rock blasting ; the plumb-bob
and a rod marked with the diameter of the hole being sufficient to insure accuracy.   Buckets, a windlass, and ropes are
required to remove the products of the excavation.   These tools
are sufficiently known to allow us to dispense with any description or illustration of them.   Where the well is sunk through
stiff clay, as, for instance, that in the London basin, steining
of half-brick thick, or four inches and a half, is required for
small wells, and of nine-inch work for wells of large diameter.
Great improvements have latterly been made in the method
of executing, and also in the stability of this description of
brickwork, owing to the use of Roman and other descriptions
of cement entirely superseding wedges of slate, bond timber,
and common mortar : the two latter are especially injurious, as
the timber will decay, and the lime in the mortar, unless it be
a blue lias or other equally hydraulic lime, will dissolve out into
the water contained in the well, rendering the same very hard ;
besides, as will be seen when describing the manner of steining, the slow setting of the mortar is a bar to its general use.
Loose wet sand, or loam, test the skill of the well-diggers : in
such cases, however, it may become necessary to puddle behind
the brickwork,* and care must be taken that the upper steining
should not slip whilst this work is being executed.   Again, in

---

* The use of puddle for any purpose of hydraulic engineering is now
nearly out of date; and it would be abandoned altogether, did our
Engineers, or Architects, insist upon the preparation of concrete in a
scientific manner.   Unfortunately this is not the case, and the real
direction of this important branch of construction is left entirely to the
care of perhaps the most uneducated class of workmen.

passing through land-springs, they must be carefully walled
out, by executing the brickwork entirely in cement—an operation which can only be accomplished when the quantity of
water entering from the spring is limited : where the rush is
enormous, as in sinking through the main sand-springs of the
plastic clay formation, the water must be dammed out, by
substituting for brickwork cylinders of iron, which may be
either cast or wrought : the latter are the more modern, and
have been applied in some large wells ; the former are the
more convenient for handling, being bolted together in seg-
ments, or in divisions. When the sinking such cylinders is
necessary, digging will most probably be precluded altogether,
and boring alone will be admissible, the cylinders sinking as
the sand is bored out : when they have been sunk to a sufficient depth in the solid clay beneath, digging and steining
may go on as before. If it be determined to bore, near
London, into the chalk, the boring should commence before
the sand-spring is entered, the expense of large cylinders
being thereby saved, as their place would be taken by the
small bore pipe ; and as the water from the chalk will generally rise higher than the level of the sand-spring itself, no
advantage is gained commensurate with the increased outlay by
sinking large cylinders. The position of the sand-spring can
be determined by boring in advance of the well itself, while the
latter is being sunk through the plastic clay : by driving a
bore-hole very small, and thus feeling the way, no danger of a
surprise may then be anticipated.

Steining is executed in a variety of ways, as regards its
manner of application, its thickness, and its bond. The bricks
used should be hard, square, and well burnt ; if the cost will
allow, malm paviours should be used, and if stocks are employed they should be the very best. As the work is for the
most part laid dry, unless the bricks run of one uniform
thickness, a great waste of time and trouble will unnecessarily
take place during the steining : again, as the bricks are laid
so as only to touch each other at the edges, a soft crumbling

brick would manifestly be useless. The old method of executing the steining was by building on a curb of wood shod
with iron. The earth being removed from the bottom, the
curb and its superstructure sunk down; the brickwork was
then added from the top, and this method of proceeding continued till the curb would sink no longer, owing to the swelling
of the ground; a new curb and new excavation smaller than
the last were then begun.

This method is now seldom used except in peculiar circumstances, all bricks being added under the executed steining,
the latter being kept from slipping by artificial means when
the natural swelling of the ground is insufficient; this circumstance is unlikely to take place when the bricks are worked close
to the sides of the excavation, in clayey soils especially; the
friction acting to prevent slipping is most enormous. The steining is usually executed partly in dry and partly in cemented
work, the latter occurring as rings laid at intervals between
the portions of the work laid dry : these are regulated by the
nature of the ground; in London clay, the intervals generally
vary from five to twelve feet, though sometimes the work
requires to be laid for some distance entirely in cement. The
rings are usually three courses thick, averaging about nine
inches in height; the bricks are laid flat, as in fig. 8, the
courses alternately breaking joint : it is often desirable to insert

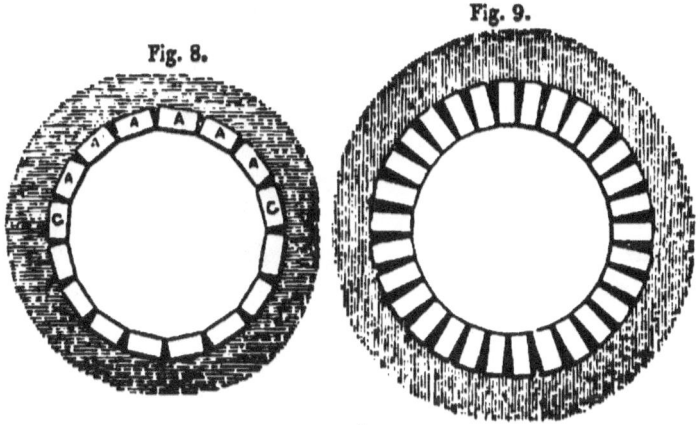

Fig. 8.   Fig. 9.

cement or small wedges in the open spaces at the back of the touching edges of the bricks.

Fig. 10

The thickness of the stein-ing itself depends on the diameter of the well and the nature of the ground to be passed through ; some use nine-inch work laid dry, and radiating as in fig. 9 : this is evidently not so strong as four-and-a-half-inch work laid in cement, or even backed with the same in the manner described above; therefore, if nine-inch work be ever used, it should be laid in cement, as being in a situation where four-and-a-half-inch work in cement will not suffice. In commen-cing an excavation from one cement ring to another, the hole is dug as far as is safe or practicable; the nature of the ground will determine this; a line is then plumbed (see fig. 10, which repre-sents a section of the stein-ing of a well) from the brickwork above, which will give the position of the face of the brickwork in the lower ring; the cement is usually gauged with half sand, as in works above ground. Too quick setting a cement is not desirable, as it partially sets in being conveyed down the well to the workmen; Roman, blue lias, Portland, or any approved water cement, may be used for the purpose. In many cases, even where the work does not absolutely require it, the steining is done entirely in cement, a practice which makes excellent work, but which is attended with a further disadvantage than the extra cost of execution, because it occasions much trouble and loss of time in fixing the permanent pumps, and temporary ones also, if any are used.

In sandy soils, should the well not be deep, the old plan of working on a curb may be adopted, but in deep wells that is inadmissible; here the steining should be set entirely in cement, and, to prevent slipping, the work should be laid in quarters, care being taken to well hang up the steining on the completion of the work by the insertion of an iron curb, secured in its place by tie-rods, which are carried up the shaft and bolted to cross timbers or another curb fixed into the brickwork. In some wells that have been executed in sandy soil, cast-iron curbs have been inserted at intervals, each curb slung to the one above it by tie-rods; the gravel or sand can then be excavated under the curb as the clay can under the brickwork rings set in cement; the curbs, in fact, bearing the same relation to the cemented brickwork, in the case of sandy soils, as the cemented rings do to the dry brickwork in clayey ground. The method of bond or laying the bricks remains to be considered: fig. 8 shows this. The bricks, though they do not touch exactly at the edges, for practically that is impossible, yet are set in but a mere trifle, and the harder the description of brick the more nearly may the edges abut; the swelling of the ground will soon fill up the spaces at the back of the edges when the bricks are laid dry: this method induces fewer joints than if the work were laid as in the manner usually adopted for half-brick arches above-ground, and for other reasons is more fit for this purpose. The ground behind them prevents any displacement of the bricks, for, the tendency of the pressure being to twist them, a compression of the ground must necessarily take place before 'movement can occur; thus the bricks, A A A, &c. in the figure, before they can be moved nearer to the centre of the well, or alter their position, must force outwards one or other of their two neighbours, G G; these cannot evidently be so moved without compressing the solid ground behind: here, again, we see the advantage of working as close as possible to such ground, and if at any time, owing to a stone or otherwise, the excavation be not perfectly round, care should be taken to puddle with solid clay behind the steining, to prevent displacement, by thus forming a sufficient abutment.

The work when 9 inches thick is laid either radiating, as in fig. 9, or in separate 4½-inch rings, fig. 11; the latter plan is usually adopted, and may be considered the best, for the following reason, it being understood that the work in both cases is laid in cement. Considering the strength as that of a compound of bricks and cement in fig. 11, fracture of the cement must take place before any failure, while in fig. 9 a slipping of the bricks away from the cement might occur; and again, in executing the work it might be considered advisable—indeed, it generally is—to execute the back steining first, for a certain distance, and afterwards to complete the inner. Even work, not wavy, but strictly vertical, constitutes good steining, and looking upwards from the bottom of a well will at once detect if the work be true or not, the eye in such case being placed close to the steining.

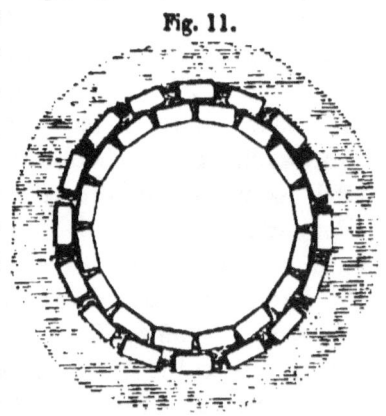

Fig. 11.

Well-diggers, after attaining a certain depth, find the confined air very unpleasant and noxious. The carbonic acid from the breath, being specifically heavier than common air, soon stagnates at the bottom of the excavation : lime-water is sometimes recommended, as this will absorb the carbonic acid ; it is, however, an awkward and unworkmanlike expedient. A pair of bellows or a fan-blast should be used in such cases, and the air conveyed down the well in pipes ; thin zinc ones answer the purpose very well ; they are about 2 inches diameter. The depth of hole at which an artificial supply of air is desirable will depend on the diameter of the well and the position of the aperture. If it be open to the air, with no temporary shed or other erection over it, a supply may not be required, with a 4-feet excavation, till about 130 feet from the surface. In this question, however, the extreme limits should not be sought for, as the sooner a plentiful supply is given the better, the workmen getting on more comfortably to them-selves, and also much more rapidly.

In the construction of iron steining the wrought-iron ones are riveted with internal ribs of angle or T-iron, so as to be flush on the outside, the rivets being countersunk to attain this end ; lowering rings are also riveted inside them, for con-venience in fixing. Cast-iron cylinders being much thicker, and therefore heavier, will sink into the hole with less driving ; they are cast in about 5-feet lengths, and are joined together with bolts and internal flanges. In sinking cylinders, their vertical position must be insured by letting them travel or slide between four battens, fixed as guides, and secured to the brickwork. When iron cylinders are used, it is generally necessary to secure up the lower part of the brickwork, as the sand and water will give it no support ; an elm or iron curb is therefore used for the purpose, which is attached by iron rods to wood beams let across the well, or iron curbs inserted some distance up the shaft. The space between the cylinders and brickwork should also be well concreted, so as to shut out the water, which would otherwise rise up from the sand. To prevent land-springs or drains from percolating into a well, it is advisable to execute the first ten or twelve feet from the surface in 9-inch work, the same being well puddled behind. When the surface soil itself is close upon the stiff clay, this may be neglected; and, when the land-springs are very strong, they must be shut out by the use of cylinders, as previously described.

CHAPTER V.

BORING.

THOUGH boring practically requires skill and care, yet in principle it is extremely simple. The operation consists, as its name would imply, in working a hole, in this case made in the crust of the earth, of a diameter varying according to circumstances, and in a vertical direction generally; not so always, however, for certain requirements may demand that it should be oblique. Many systems have been and now are practised in carrying on this kind of work; and though in England but one is usually followed,—of many modifications, it is true,—yet it would be well to mention one or two other plans. The simplest is that practised in various parts of the Continent, and called the Chinese system; here all rods connected to the boring-tool in the ordinary plan are dispensed with, the borer being suspended by a rope, which, when the tool is worked vertically up and down, imparts by its torsion a sufficient circular motion to the tool. In this case the tool and the rope are surrounded by an iron cylinder, and the products of the excavation become collected in the circular space between the tool and the cylinder, by which means they may be brought up to the surface of the ground. With so simple a machine, different tools, of course, being used for various strata, it may be asked, why has this plan not superseded all others? Now, where simplicity can be gained without corresponding disadvantage, it is well to employ it; but where a manifest inferiority exists, to choose simplicity in opposition to complexity, for its own sake alone, is absurd. To this plan one serious drawback occurs, which is, that the bore-hole is apt to become crooked, so that a great difficulty, if not impossibility, would take place in sinking the pipes necessary for protecting the hole. That this fault could be rectified there can be little doubt; but until this is done, the system of boring by impact alone, assisted by the twisting action of the rope, will never become very general. In rocky strata, or in places where the straightness of the hole is of little moment, this method may be applied.

The ordinary plan is to attach the borer, which differs according to the nature of the work to be done, to iron rods screwed together in lengths of from ten to twenty feet; a circular motion being given to the borer by the workmen above, assisted when required by a vertical jumping motion, causes the boring-tool to work for itself a hole in the ground. It is evident that by this plan a great loss of time is entailed, for the tool, when it becomes full of the products of the boring, must be drawn up to the boring stage, to be emptied of its contents, and to effect this the rods must be unscrewed. This unscrewing and screwing, pulling up and letting down, is an operation, entailing a great loss of time, which it would be important to supersede. An apparatus has been proposed to accomplish this object, and was patented by Beart in the year 1844. The rod connecting the boring-tool with the workmen above is hollow, forming a tube with water-tight joints; into this tube water is introduced, an upward and downward current of the same being gained by allowing the water to flow in one direction in the tube, and in the other in the circular space around it. The strength of this current the inventor considers sufficient to carry up with it the materials which are loosened by the boring-tool. That some loose matter could be so carried is probable, though in a majority of cases it is likely it might be impossible. Another objection to this arrangement is the immense quantity of water necessary, an article which, in sinking a well, is not usually very plentiful until obtained from the well itself.*

Confining ourselves, therefore, to the ordinary system, it will be proper, in the first place, to notice a few prepara-tions which are necessary before commencing the boring itself. Assuming a well to be sunk so deep that we are certain that when the spring is tapped the water will rise a sufficient distance within it, the first consideration will be, can the boring take place from some point in the well itself, or must we work from the surface? The answer to this will depend on the depth of the proposed bore, together with its diameter, and the nature of the ground to be worked into. If the well be under 4 feet diameter, it is difficult to obtain sufficient leverage for any heavy work, if the boring takes place from a point in the well distant from the surface of the ground: in that case we are driven to work from the surface, but, where it is possible to bore from below, it is better to do so for the following reasons, among others: first, there will be a great saving of temporary work above-ground, for the stage the workmen bore from must, if above-ground, be elevated some distance from the surface—20 feet at least—or great waste of time will take place in screwing and unscrewing the rods, &c.; secondly, a less weight of rods will be on the windlass, for, if the boring takes place from a point in the well, the rods need only to be suspended by ropes from the windlass to the stage in the well from which the boring takes place; and there will be an economy of time in screwing and unscrewing the rods, as they may be drawn up without detaching them from each other in lengths equal to the distance of the windlass to the boring

* The system described above was first brought prominently before the public by M. Arago, as the invention of a M. Fauvel. Notwithstand-ing the countenance of that Philosopher and of Dr. Buckland, the objections cited in the text are valid; and practically it has been shown that the system could not be worked. At any rate it has been allowed to drop quietly.—G. R. B.

stage nearly. To reap the same advantage when boring from the surface, a high pair of sheers or a triangle is requisite, which, of course, adds to the expense and trouble.

Supposing it decided that boring should be carried on in the well, care should be taken to fix on the position of the stage or floor from which the work is done; this should be as low as practicable, as may be supposed from what has been said before; but at the same time the stage should be a sufficient distance above the level in the well to which the water will rise. This is a consideration which can be ascertained only by experience and a knowledge of the spring-water level of the district. The stage consists of a stout plank floor, resting on strong putlocks. The flooring is well braced together by planks nailed transversely across the same. In the centre of this floor is a square hole, a little larger than the boring-rods, which therefore can pass through it, but not large enough to allow a small hook apparatus, represented in fig. 15, p. 44, which, having the power of holding the rods suspended while they are screwed and unscrewed, will prevent their falling through the stage. From the bottom of the well to above where the water will rise, say to nearly under the boring stage, wooden trunks, strongly but temporarily secured, are fixed as guides for the boring-tools, permanent pipes, &c. These trunks may be made square, and are fitted by sockets one into the other. Sometimes temporary iron pipes are used instead of these wooden trunks. The permanent pipe to be inserted in the hole bored should be joined together and slung down the well, ready to be fixed when occasion may require. Thus having, we will suppose, bored through the mottled clay, the sooner the pipes follow the better, as the sand underneath is liable to blow up into the bore-hole, or the clay itself, when not dense and stiff, may fall, and to a certain extent choke up the hole. These pipes are either of cast or wrought iron; the latter are generally used for small distances, and the former, as being thicker, for very deep work, where much driving will be required. The lower pipes of the series are usually perforated with small holes when the spring is a sand one; but, when the water is to rise from chalk or rock, no perforation is required, because the pipes themselves are only requisite when the bore-hole will not stand without them. In many cases in and about London, advantage is taken both of the main sand spring and the chalk springs also; then perforated pipes are driven in the former, smaller pipes and a smaller bore being continued to the chalk. The junctions of the pipes show nearly, sometimes quite, an even face on the outside. The cast-iron ones have generally turned joints and wrought-iron collars, usually flush on the inside as well as on the outside; if, however, required to be slighter, they may be cast with the vertical portion of a less thickness than the flanges; for if the thickness at the joint be the same in both cases, no advantage, as far as passing tools up and down, is gained by having the internal diameter uniform throughout, though there is a great advantage in point of strength. The collars are sometimes fixed on the pipes with screws; though, when the joints are not turned, they are run together with metal: this latter plan will entirely exclude any bad water which may be met with; but the other mode of fixing is the one usually adopted. The wrought-iron pipes are now seldom riveted, but have thin collars soldered on to the pipes, which are never quite flush outside. The melting of the solder, previously run into the parts to be joined, is accomplished by suspending iron heaters down the pipe; the small heater being made of one, and the larger heater of two, circular pieces of iron.

The pipes are lowered into the well by means of a wooden plug traversed on the under-side by pins or keys of sufficient length to carry the sides of the pipe. A small groove is cut in the pipe to receive these keys, and as soon as the pipe is lowered into its place it may be detached from the plug by merely turning the latter in a direction which will cause the keys to fall back into the depressions, or seats, left for the purpose of bringing them within the dimensions of the interior of the pipe. By means of these keys it is also possible to drive the pipes, by causing them to bear upon its upper end. (See fig. 24, p. 50.)

The boring-rods are usually made of wrought iron, in lengths of from 10 to 20 feet; it is, however, convenient to employ them of only one length, and to number the rods, in order at any time to have an approximate guide to the depth of the boring. The head of the first rod is made with a hook, by means of which it is suspended to the lever communicating

Fig. 12. Fig. 13. Fig. 14.

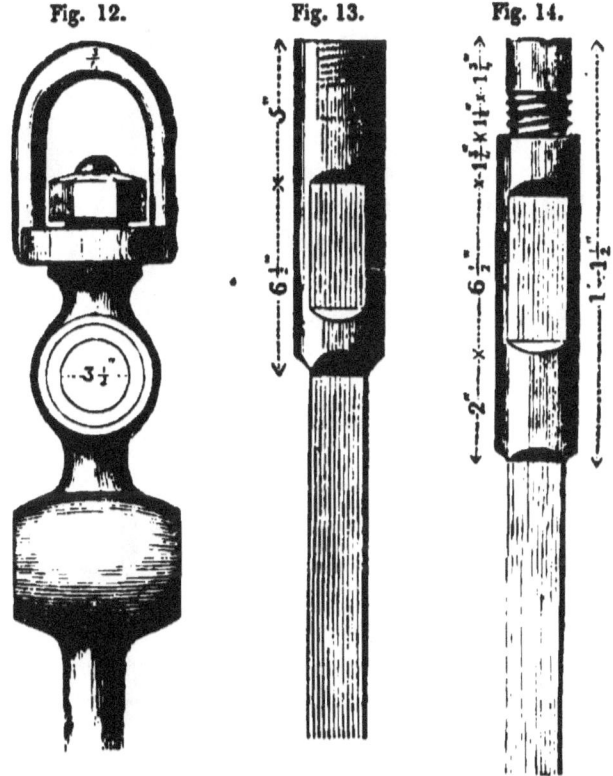

Head and joints of iron rods.

the percussive motion; and below this hook it has an eye formed to receive a transverse bar, which, by being turned by the workmen, communicates the rotary motion (see fig. 12). The bottom of each rod has a socket, tapped with a female

screw, to receive the head of the succeeding rod, which is
formed by a male screw fitting into the socket.   Under the
screwed head there is a swelling out of the rod, indicated in
fig. 13, for the purpose of suspending it during the operation
of withdrawal; the projection rests upon the sides of the
crow's foot (fig. 15), whilst the upper
rod being detached, and the crow's foot
itself is supported by the stage upon which
the men work.

Fig. 15.

In borings of small depth the rotary
and percussive motions are produced by
manual labour; when the depth becomes
exceedingly great, however, horse-power,
or the steam engine, must be employed,
on account of the weight of the rods.   In
sinking the wells at Grenelle, M. Mulot
used a horse-mill; of late years M..De-
gousée has employed steam, and at Southampton latterly the rods were raised and
lowered by steam-power.

The rotary motion is usually commu-
nicated by means of levers traversing the
eye in the position shown in fig. 12, as
before stated; and in tolerably yielding
materials, such as clay, sand, soft chalk,
&c., no other motion is required to secure
the descent of the boring-tool; but in
harder materials it is necessary to com-
minute the rock before the tool can make

any progress.   The simplest manner of
effecting this object consists in suspending
the rods by a rope coiled two or three
times round the barrel of a windlass, and
adjusting the rope in such a manner that if a workman hold
one end of the coil tight the friction will be sufficient to raise
the rods on the windlass being set in motion.   Should the end

of the rope the workman holds now be slackened, the coil becomes loose, and the rods descend with a force proportionate to their own weight and the distance they have travelled through. A regular percussive action is therefore gained by keeping the windlass constantly in motion in one direction, the attending workman alternately allowing the rods to be drawn up a certain distance, and then, by relaxing his hold, to fall.

From this description of the manner of communicating the different movements to the rods it must be evident that their weight is a very important consideration, and that in order to resist the efforts of torsion and percussion they must be made of dimensions proportionate to the depth of the bore. For depths not exceeding 100 feet, and with a bore-hole of from 2 to 3 inches, a rod 1 inch square, weighing 3½ lbs. per foot lineal will suffice. A depth of about from 600 to 700 feet, with a bore-hole of 6 or 7 inches diameter, will require rods measuring at least 1¾ inch on a side, weighing 8·8 lbs. per foot lineal; whilst for such depths as the wells at Grenelle or Southampton they would require to be at least 2 inches on the side and weigh 13½ lbs. per foot. The weight thus increases as rapidly as the depth; and when the latter is considerable, inasmuch as the upper parts bear upon the working end, the danger of rupture also augments.

At very great depths not only does the weight of the rods become an evil of serious importance, but when the percussive motion is given to the rods they vibrate with great force, and striking against the sides of the bore, they are likely to detach portions of the rock, which would, in that case, fall upon the top of the tool. This danger has been sometimes obviated by using lighter and more voluminous rods; indeed, as the bore-holes are usually filled with water, and therefore the rods lose a portion of their weight, it is advantageous to increase the volume, even if the weight remain the same. M. Degousée effected the desired object by using wooden rods surrounded by iron bands, and with iron screwed heads (see fig. 16); or by using tubular wrought-iron rods of the same weight per foot lineal as the solid rods, but which, owing to their displacement of water, did not act so injuriously upon the lower portions, whilst, at the same time, their volume rendered them less liable to vibrations. The wrought-iron tubes present this advantage over the wooden rods, that they are more calculated to resist the effort of torsion; but the latter, on the contrary, are lighter.

Beyond a certain depth it is dangerous to exercise a percussive action of such power as to expose the lower rods to be broken. Many accidents have occurred in borings from the neglect of this consideration, and perhaps the well of Grenelle furnished a greater number of illustrations of the necessity for the abstract theoretical calculations of the weight and description of the rods to be employed than any well ever executed; it was marked by a continued series of accidents from this cause. Indeed, when borings exceed 1000 feet, the systems above described, viz. the use of wooden or tubular rods, will not suffice to obviate the danger of crushing the lower portions of the boring-tool, and the slide-joint, invented by Œuyenhausen, is necessary to insure their safety.

When this joint is used the rod is divided into two portions; the upper one being counterbalanced by a weight suspended to a lever, and the lower one only allowed to act by percussion,—the weight of the latter rarely exceeding from 12 to 16 cwt. Between these portions the slide-joint is introduced. It consists of two parts (see fig. 17) able to slide upon one another for a distance of about one foot, and so arranged that during the descent one becomes detached from the other. The upper part is balanced by the counterpoise. When the boring-tool is allowed to descend after it has been

Fig. 16.

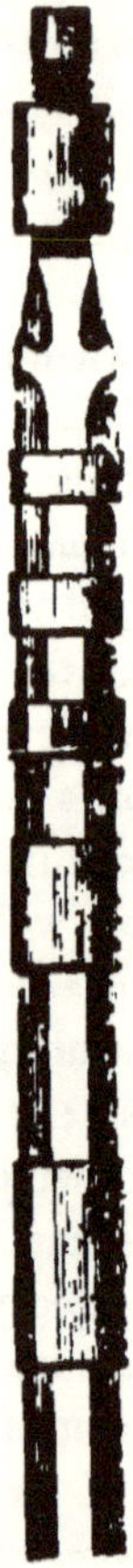

Wooden rod, bound with iron.

raised for the purpose of getting the blow, it will strike the bottom simply with a weight equal to that of the lower portion, and the upper portion will descend gently through the distance of 1 foot until it rests upon the collar. Should it be required to bore without percussion, the slide-joint is suppressed, and a common rod substituted; in that case also the lighter and weaker rods are replaced by stout bars able to resist an effort of torsion.

As the boring-tool is in all these operations the acting part, its form varies according to the object proposed to be attained and the resistance of the ground to be traversed; the first condition being that it correspond with the diameter of the bore. Each tool is shut upon a rod carrying a joint, the joint being usually a screw, with the female screw downwards. The boring-tools may be divided into four classes, according to the object they are intended to effect: 1. tools for cutting or comminuting rocks by percussion (see figs. 18, 19, 20); 2. tools for extracting soft or disintegrated materials (see figs. 21, 22, 23); 3. tools for cleansing and enlarging, or equalizing the bore-hole; 4. tools for extracting any broken rods, or for accidental works, or for raising or lowering the tubes.

The tools for percussion consist of an infinite number of chisels whose forms do not appear to require so many modifications as workmen usually introduce. In hard rocks, such as the oolites, a plain chisel with a diameter equal to the hole to be bored, and with a cutting edge, is sufficient. The shape represented in figs. 18 and 19 is adapted to harder rocks, such as the sandstones, because it divides the action. The twisted chisel, fig. 20, is adapted for softer rocks.

Fig. 17.

Œuyenhausen's slide-joint.

Boring-tools are usually made upon the same principle as
wood augers; that is to say, they consist of a point which
disintegrates the rock by its rotary motion; of a species of
tongue, or occasionally of a clack, to support the loosened

Figs. 18, 19, 20. Chisels.

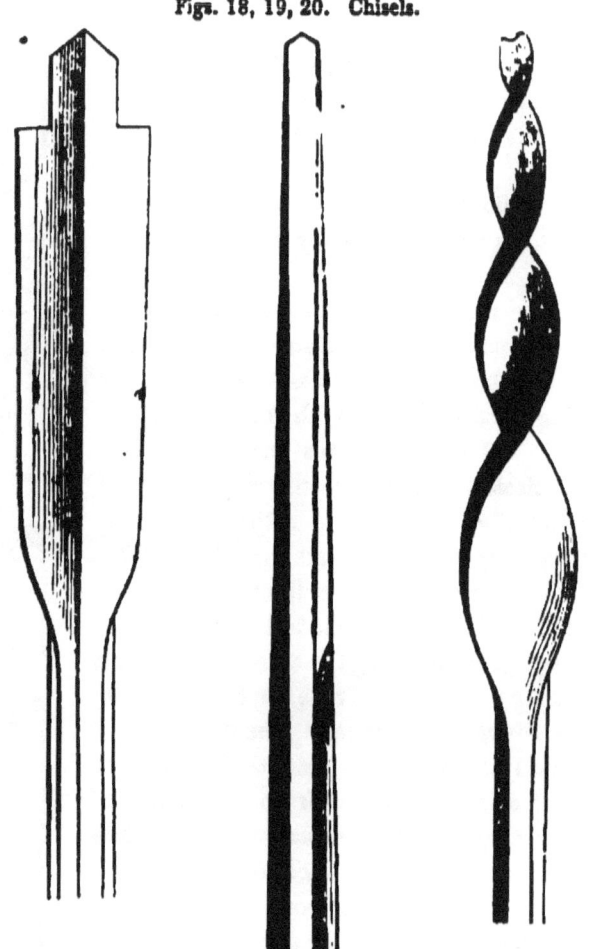

materials; and of the body of the auger, which contains these
materials, at the same time that it serves to enlarge the hole.
It must be evident that these augers can only be used in soft

ground, for they would not exercise any action upon hard rocks. Their forms differ according to the nature of the strata traversed, being open and cylindrical, in clayey or cal-

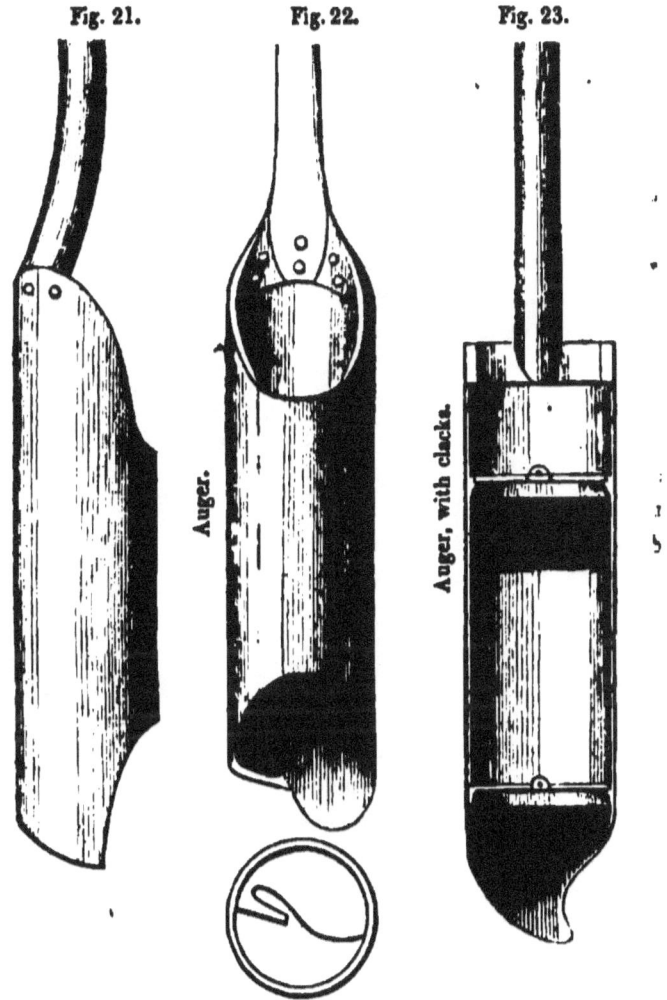

Fig. 21.   Fig. 22.   Fig. 23.

Auger.   Auger, with clacks.

careous lands possessing a certain degree of cohesion. They are closed, and sometimes conical, in running sands; and in this case it is also necessary occasionally to use closed augers with clacks, or even a moveable bullet, to preve:.t the accumulated matters from falling back into the bore.

The tools used for enlarging a hole may consist either of the chisel (Nos. 18, 19) already described, or of augers with increasing diameters. M. Degouscé used a very simple tool for the purpose of equalizing the dimensions of a bore, which consisted of two iron plates, from 5 to 7 feet apart, between which square bars with cutting edges were inserted vertically. These bars, if made to turn in the hole, would of course act upon the sides for their whole height.

The tools for the purpose of withdrawing any broken rods consist of three principal descriptions: a species of hook which is made to fit under the projecting parts of the rod; a screw tap, the mouth of which is larger than the end of the rod to be raised; and a spring clutch, so arranged that the rod will allow the catches to descend, but in the upward motion they are pressed upon the rod by means of steel springs. Should these means fail, no resource is left but to thrust the rod aside, into the bore, and continue the work beyond it. Fig. 25 represents a tool occasionally used to withdraw broken portions of rods.

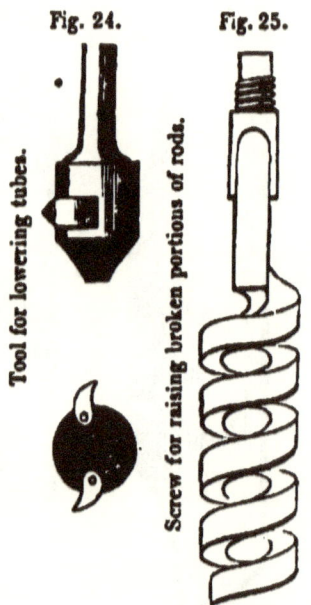

Fig. 24.   Fig. 25.

Tool for lowering tubes.

Screw for raising broken portions of rods.

The scotch, fig. 26, is used for the purpose of allowing the rods to rest on the wooden stage, or for that of unscrewing the different lengths. The tool represented by fig. 24 is for the purpose of lowering tubes into their places; when open, the tongues bear against pins upon the bottom of the tubes; by turning in a reverse direction, they fall back into the seats prepared to receive them; this tool has been already referred to; another instrument for effecting the same purpose will be found at page 84.

Fig. 26.

Scotch.

It must not be understood that the above description comprehends every tool used by well-borers. Each contractor, in fact, has his own system, and the nature of the ground to be operated upon varies so much in one locality from what it is in another, that every case requires to be treated, as it were, upon its own merits. In M. Degousée's work will be found ample illustrations of the various tools he has employed in his extensive practice; and the reader who would desire further information upon this subject is referred to it, and to Burat's 'Geologie appliquée à la Recherche des Minéraux utiles.'

The vertical position of the rods is insured by attaching to them four guides fitting closely into the bore-hole, yet allowing the free action of the tools themselves.

CHAPTER VI.

VARIOUS METHODS OF RAISING WATER.

As it is desirable to make this work as practical as possible, the space which might be taken up in describing methods of raising water in ancient times, or those proposed in our own, but which, practically, have not superseded the pump, or common windlass and bucket, is passed over. All elementary books on hydrostatics and hydraulics contain descriptions of Archimedean screws, endless bands, Jacob's ladders, Persian wheels, &c.; to such works the reader must therefore be referred. The common bucket and windlass is the simplest arrangement for raising water from wells, and, in parts of the country where wells are deep, is used in preference to pumps. except where a large quantity of water is required; for, as will be presently shown, the common pump will not draw water more than 30 or 33 feet at most,—sometimes, taking imperfections into account, not more than 25,—while the deep well pump, from its situation, rods, rising main, &c., is a more expensive affair than the bucket and windlass. In some districts the springs are within a few feet of the surface; here a pole with a hook at the end, to which the bucket is attached, supplies the place of the rope and windlass. Where a windlass is used, it can be worked either by hand or by horse or donkey power, the horse-wheel working either horizontally, as in the case of a pug or clay mill, or vertically, the animal working from inside the wheel or drum. Often the windlass, though worked by hand, is driven by second motion, a spur-wheel situated on it, gearing into a pinion fixed on the axle, to which the winch is attached. Examples of the above methods of raising water are common in parts of Hertfordshire; they answer very well for small quantities of water periodically required, but for filling cisterns or reservoirs, &c. are of little use, and for such purposes pumps are always adopted.

The principle of the pump is very simple; in its most common form, the pump consists of a barrel truly cylindrical, into which fits the sliding portion of the pump, or bucket, as it is called. This bucket has a valve in it opening upwards; a similar valve, also opening upwards, is situated at the bottom of the barrel, which is called the sucker. The action of the pump is as follows: when the bucket is drawn up in the barrel, into which it fits air-tight, a partial vacuum will be formed under it, more or less complete according to the perfection of the apparatus; the valve in the bucket will be kept shut by the pressure of the air above it, while the valve in the sucker will be forced upwards by the water rising into the barrel, which water is forced into the vacuum under the bucket by the air pressing on the exposed surface in the well; in other words, by abstracting the pressure of the air from off part of the surface of the water, that portion under the bucket is forced upwards by the pressure on the remaining portion of its surface, just as, in compressing a bladder full of any liquid, the latter will gush out at any aperture, there being little or no resistance at that point. Supposing the up-stroke of the bucket complete, and the space under it charged with water, on commencing the down-stroke the water cannot return downwards through the sucker, for the valve in it will be shut by the weight of the water, but the valve in the bucket will be raised by the same effort; thus the position of the water will be changed from under to over the bucket. It is manifest that, on the up-stroke of the bucket, the water resting above it can be raised to any height required; but the height to which the water under the bucket can be thus raised above the natural level of the well is limited by a law of nature within the range of from 30 to 33 feet, before stated. The explanation is as follows: the pressure of the air on the surface of the water balances a column of the latter in the suction-pipe; it follows, that if the height of the pipe be such that the column of water equals in weight that of a column of air of the same diameter, and of the total height of the atmosphere, the column of water would be pressed upwards no longer, for the two weights would be in equilibrium. That the comparison should be made with a column of air of the diameter of the pump, and not the total weight of the air pressing on the whole surface of the water in the well, will be understood by imagining for a moment the effect of having a pipe one square inch in area, and of length sufficient to contain a quantity of water greater in weight than that of a column of air also one square inch in area, and of the total height of the atmosphere: on filling this with water, its lower end being open and immersed in the well, the effect would be that the pressure on the square inch under the pipe would be greater than the pressure per square inch of the air on any other part of the surface of the water in the well. The particles of the water, from their extreme mobility, would transmit this in all directions; the extra pressure per square inch being divided equally throughout the mass, would re-act against the total atmospheric pressure, causing the latter to yield;

the general level of the water will rise from the additional quantity running in, and this will continue until there is an equilibrium of pressure per square inch between the water in the pipe, pressing on the surface of the water in the well, and the pressure of the atmosphere. A comparison of the relative weights of water and air would appear to warrant our placing the sucker of a pump at a greater height above the surface of the water in the well than is usually adopted in practice; but the imperfections of the different parts of the machinery do not admit of its ever being carried beyond from 25 to 28 feet at the utmost.

Forcing pumps are used when the height to which the water has to be raised exceeds the above limits, and they may be of two kinds, viz. pumps in which the column of water which has already passed through the piston is lifted by it, or pumps which have valves at the feet of their rising mains, through which the water is forced at the down-stroke of the piston. At great depths the former description is never employed, because it would be necessary to lift the whole column of water at the up-stroke of the pump. When the latter is used, it is customary to combine the suction and the forcing principles as far as possible, in order to diminish the weight to be raised.

Generally speaking, the suction tube is placed immediately under the working part of the pump, in the same straight line, and the rising main is placed by the side. Sometimes, however, the pipes are made continuous, and the pump is upon the side; and in other combinations a single piston is made, both to raise the water by suction, and to force it into the rising main at each up and down stroke of the piston.

When a greater quantity of water is required to be discharged with a continuous flow than the well or spring is able to furnish, it is important to place the end of the pump under the surface of the water, so as to insure a good reservoir at starting. The following Table, containing the number of gallons for every foot in depth in wells of different diameters, will be found to be useful in many calculations respecting their yield:

Diameter.		Contents in gallons.		Diameter.		Contents in gallons.
2	0	19¼		5	0	122
2	6	30½		6	0	176
3	0	44		7	0	239
3	6	60		8	0	313
4	0	78		9	0	396
4	6	100		10	0	489

In the plunger pump the bucket is dispensed with, and in its place a solid cylindrical plunger slides air-tight through a stuffing-box. The up-stroke of the plunger will cause a partial vacuum in the pump-barrel, and water will therefore rise into it through the lower clack. The barrel of the pump communicates with another and similar clack opening upwards; the down-stroke of the plunger will therefore force the water from the barrel of the pump through this valve, which, of course, by shutting, prevents the water returning to the pump. In addition to many other reasons for employing this pump in certain situations, the little trouble in attending to the packing, compared with the removal of the buckets for the purpose of putting fresh leathers on the clacks of the other descriptions of pumps, causes it to be a great favourite with workmen.

More pumps are usually used in well-work than one, except in very small wells, where the motive power is manual, and acting on an ordinary pump-handle: where that or any other force acts through the medium of wheel-work, the irregularity of motion caused by the varying resistance of the pump is so great as to require the effort to be regulated either by placing a counterweight so as to render the up and down stroke of the pump uniform in resistance, or to fix more than one pump. The nearest approach to equality of resistance takes place when three pumps are used, worked by an axle having three cranks set at an angle of 120° with each other. When the power applied to them is uniform, and not governed by a fly-wheel, this arrangement is worthy of adoption. But a serious objection exists with respect to the use of three pumps on the score of expensiveness, and the increased friction arising from the three barrels, buckets and rods; so that, whenever it is possible, it will be found advisable to employ two pumps and to equalize the effort exerted upon them by means of a fly-wheel. The above remarks, it must be remembered, only apply to pumps worked through the intervention of wheel-work.

In the case of large pumping engines, which act directly on the pumps themselves, all the details of the subject are altered. It sometimes is desirable, in very deep wells, to raise the water in separate lifts, that is, the pumps are situated at various heights up the shaft; the lowermost one supplies a cistern from which the pump directly above it draws, and this in like manner feeds the pump situated in the next lift. The advantage of this arrangement is obvious. Each pump has a comparatively small weight of water to raise; a lesser strain is thereby occasioned, and in case of any leakage of the clacks or buckets, its effect is not so disadvantageously felt. The materials of which pumps are made differ, they being either of wood, lead, iron, brass, or gunmetal. Wooden pumps are now nearly out of date; leaden pumps, with wooden buckets and suckers, are extensively used for shallow wells, raising water from ponds, reservoirs, &c.; iron pumps are also used for the same purpose, and also for fixing in deep wells; they are inferior to brass or gunmetal, as being more liable to corrosion, but they are cheaper, and experience has shown them not to corrode so rapidly as might be supposed; indeed, it is not so much in the barrels of the pumps that corrosion takes place (water alone having no oxidating power) as in the rods, nuts, screws, and other parts exposed to the joint action of air and water. Pump-rods are either of copper or iron; copper is the best, but the dearest, the iron ones corroding very fast, especially where

they pass through the guides: the junctions of the rods are
scarfed and secured by brass or iron ferrules. The rods can be
thus readily taken asunder by merely loosening the ferrules,
which is effected by driving them with a hammer upwards.
The guides for keeping the rods strictly vertical are either
made of wooden cleats, or of brass rollers bolted to cross timbers ; the former plan is the simplest, and by many considered
as the best, for, the guides being inexpensive, it is usual to
place more of them than when rollers are used, and is, therefore, usually adopted. Formerly the distance between these
guides exceeded the present practice, but experience has
shown that a distance of six feet is the most advantageous
where the works are not on a large scale.

In computing the quantity of water a pump will throw at a
given velocity, and the power required to work it, the following
memoranda will be found useful:

Weight of Water, &c.

1 cubic foot	.	.	.	.	62·5 lbs.
1 cubic foot	.	.	.	.	6·25 gallons nearly.
1 gallon	.	.	.	.	10·0 lbs. about.
1·8 cubic foot	.	.	.	.	1 cwt.
35·84 cubic feet	.	.	.	.	1 ton.
11· 2 gallons	.	.	.	.	1 cwt.
224· 0 gallons	.	.	.	.	1 ton.
277·274 cubic inches	.	.	.	.	1 gallon.

The quantity of water thrown by a pump will equal the
cubical contents of the space in the pump-barrel comprised in
one stroke of the bucket, multiplied by the number in any
given time ; this is evident, as in one stroke a quantity is
discharged equal in diameter to the barrel, and in length
equal to the play of the bucket. Thus, suppose a pump 3
inches diameter, 9-inch stroke of bucket, working 27 strokes
per minute,—required the quantity of water delivered? To
find the contents of the pump we have to square the diameter × by ·7854 and then by the length of stroke: 3 sq.
= 9 × ·7854 = 7·0686 for the area (say to occupy less

space, neglecting the decimals, 7); 7 multiplied by 9, the length of stroke, = 63 cubic inches, for the capacity of one stroke, 63 × 27 = 1701 cubic inches, or very nearly a cubic foot, which is 1728 cubic inches, that is, very nearly 6¼ gallons. The above calculation, when applied to large pumps, would have all the terms in feet instead of inches. In ascertaining the power necessary for working the same, it must be borne in mind that the resistance opposed to motion is the friction of the bucket and other moving parts, the weight of the rods unless they are counterbalanced, and the weight of the water moved. The weight of the latter, whatever be the diameter of the pipes to or from the pump, is equal to that of a cylindrical column, the diameter of the pump-barrel, and in height equal to the distance from the surface of the water in the well to that of the reservoir into which it is delivered; in other words, the total height raised. The friction of the working parts depends on various circumstances, and that of the water on the material and size of the rising main, suction pipes, &c.: one-fifth the total weight of water is usually allowed for friction, and though it is manifestly absurd to so make it a fraction of the weight of the water, when it really depends on other matters, yet the above rule is sufficiently accurate in practice to insure adequate power.

The above calculation only applies to the resistance to motion; that, together with the speed at which the work is done, really is the test of the power required : multiplying, therefore, the total resistance by the speed per foot per minute that the pump-bucket raises the water, the result will be an amount by which to compare the relative power of the prime mover, whose useful effect multiplied into its speed per foot per minute must exceed that of the work done. Commercially it is allowed that a dead weight of 33,000 ℔s., raised one foot per minute, shall equal a horse-power; a comparison is therefore at once established by which to measure the work, and also to provide the power. We will proceed to apply the above datum to the preceding example, and suppose the total height the water is to be raised is 99 feet. The following consideration will be useful, viz.: on squaring the diameter of a pipe in inches, the product will be the number of pounds of water avoirdupois contained in every yard of pipe.

In 99 feet are 33 yards, which, multiplied by 3 squared, or 9 = 297 lbs. The bucket makes 27 strokes per minute, moving the column of water each stroke 9″, in all 27 × 9″ = 243 inches, or 20 feet 3 inches per minute, and multiplying the resistance, 297 lbs. × 20 speed in feet per minute, we have = 5940 lbs., moved over one foot per minute. Add for friction, say 1000 lbs., and 6940 will equal the momentum required in the prime mover, or rather more than one-fifth of a horse-power.

Should it be required to know whether a man, acting on a winch connected by wheel-work with the above pump, can work it, the comparison is easily made. Suppose the revolutions made by the winch 50 per minute, the distance travelled by it in one revolution four feet, and the man's force continually acting throughout the revolution to be a pressure equal to 40 lbs.; we have 40, the force, multiplied by 4, the distance of one revolution, equal to 160 multiplied by 50, the number of revolutions, equal to 8000 lbs., moving over one foot per minute,—an amount quite sufficient to work the pump.

The size of the pumps and number of them being determined, the prime mover is the next question. In all cases where a continuous supply of water is required, or where large cisterns are to be filled, manual labour, even for small pumps, will be found the worst and dearest. Water-power is seldom, for obvious reasons, applicable. Wind can sometimes be applied, and, where it can be depended on, will supersede all others; but it is only in peculiar situations that it can be trusted. The above motive powers, however, all give place to steam, which can be used under all circumstances. On a large scale, the use of steam is sufficiently extensive; but its advantages in superseding manual labour in filling cisterns, &c.

have not hitherto been sufficiently appreciated. The work
can be done much more rapidly, and it is nearly self-evident
that, even with such a small-sized pump as the one alluded to
in the foregoing examples, a man's time is better applied in
tending a small engine for three or four hours than in slaving
like a machine for double or treble the time. It is clear he
must rest, while the engine never tires; and equally so, that
he who tends the engine is, after pumping, an intelligent
servant, fit for other work, while he who performs the func-
tions of a machine is, by the very nature of the work, unfitted
for any higher occupation.

When pumps are applied to an existing horse-wheel—I say
existing, for few now choose horse-power in preference to steam,
unless the wheel is already erected—the number of revolutions
of the wheel should, by a train of toothed wheels, be so pro-
portioned as to work the pumps at the speed best suited to
them. This velocity depends greatly on the size of the suction
and delivery pipes; the larger the pipes, the quicker may be
the motion. The size of the pumps, and the height of the lifts,
must be taken into account. When pumps work too quickly,
they are apt to jerk, and are sure to strike their clacks, with
great force, into their seats; when too slowly, the motion of
the pump becomes quivering. The following examples may
be cited to illustrate the variations of speed admitted in
practice:

Situation.	Size of pump.	No. of effect-ive strokes.
Hampstead Water-Works . .	2'·3" stroke . 9" diam.	. . 15
Kilburn Brewery.	9 „ . 3 „	. . 18
Camden Station	2·0 „ . 8 inches	. . 20
Kingsbury	8 „ . 3" diam.	. . 24

When steam is applied to pumping, if the machine be large
enough, it should be applied directly to the pump, or through
the intervention of a beam alone: this arrangement is adopted
in the ordinary pumping engine, both with forcing and lifting
pumps. The motion of the Cornish engine is single-acting,

that is to say, the steam only acts on the piston during its down-stroke, the weight of the pump-rods, &c. acting on the opposite end of the beam, completing its up-stroke. The single-acting engine has one disadvantage when working a single-lifting pump, situated in a deep well; that is, a certain amount of power is consumed in raising the pump-rods; and this can be obviated in many ways. The one generally adopted is as follows: the work being divided, say into two lifts, for the lower a lifting-pump is used, and for the upper a forcing or plunger pump, similar in principle to the feed-pump of a steam boiler. The acting stroke of the plunger being the down-stroke, the power required in previously lifting the pump-rods is not lost, inasmuch as in their down-stroke the power is returned to the work. The up and down stroke of the piston may be thus represented, omitting friction: the down-stroke of the piston raises the pump-rods and weight of water on the lower lift, and on the upper lift as far as the plunger-pump sucker; the down-stroke of the pump-rods raises the piston, and forces the water from the plunger-pump to the top of the lift: thus, in effect, the only work done, if the lifts be so arranged, is in raising the water, and an amount of counterbalance sufficient for raising the steam piston. When plunger-pumps are used, wrought-iron rods are dispensed with, the rods being in a state of compression, and if of wrought iron, unless inconveniently large, would spring and buckle; wooden rods or poles are therefore adopted. Cast-iron ones have been tried, but not with the same success as wood, taking into consideration the relative strength, lightness, and durability of the two materials. When small pumps are worked by steam, the plan of engine above alluded to is seldom used, on account of the complication, first cost, and wear and tear: a steam engine of the ordinary construction, working the pumps at a less velocity than the steam piston, is found to answer the purpose better, though an increased expenditure of fuel is attendant on the choice. Sometimes the speed is brought down by intervening wheel-work, as illustrated by the engine at the Hampstead Water-Works,

Hampstead Heath, and also by the engine at the well at Kings-
bury. At other times the speed of the pumps is reduced from
that of the steam piston, by giving the latter a longer stroke
than the pump-buckets or plungers have. An example of this
is to be found in the works at the Camden Station.

When a well is completed as regards its digging, steining,
boring, fixing of pumps, engine, &c., the care of the works is
a matter of more importance than owners usually think.
Periodical visits should be paid to the pumps, for the purpose
of ascertaining their condition, and keeping in order the clacks,
buckets, stuffing-boxes, and various moving parts, greasing
such as require lubrication, &c. A permanent windlass should
always be fixed, or iron ladders, to give access to the well.
An apparatus for blowing fresh air down the well, if it is at all
deep, should be provided ; and the simplest machine for this
purpose is a kind of wooden air-pump, consisting of a vertical
square box, open at the top, and at the bottom connected to
pipes leading down the well. In this box, loosely fitting,
slides a piston, or pump-bucket, made of a piece of flat wood,
with one or more holes, covered on the under-side by a leather
flap, or valve, which opens a little way downwards. During
the up-stroke of this bucket, the air merely changes its position from the top to the under-side of the bucket; during the
down-stroke the valve or flap closes; the air, therefore, will
be forced down the pipe leading to the well. In addition to
these, some method should be adopted for ascertaining the
water-level, which varies, generally, by the pumping; a float
on the water, attached to a wire, which, in its turn, is secured
to a string passing round a pulley, will suffice for this purpose.
A pressure gauge, such as that used for a steam boiler, is the
most perfect arrangement for this purpose, though more expensive. The mode of application consists in leading a pipe from
the gauge down to the bottom of the water in the well. If this
pipe be filled with air, by means of a small pump, the air will
necessarily be compressed more or less, according to the height
of water above the aperture of the pipe. This compressed air,

re-acting on the mercury in the gauge, will correctly measure the depth of water. Were it not for leakage, and the absorption of the air by the water, the pump would not be necessary, the pipe alone would suffice.

CHAPTER VII.

NOTES ON WELL-WORK ALREADY EXECUTED.

BEFORE proceeding to offer any remarks on this portion of our subject, it may be desirable to place before the reader the following specifications, one of which was used by the late Mr. Swindell for a well only, and the other for a work comprising both well-digging and boring.

Conditions and particulars to be observed by the contractor during the sinking, steining, and boring a well, situate at ————, for ————, and to be executed under the super-intendence of Mr. J. G. Swindell, architect, of No. 3, Kilburn Priory.

The work to be carried steadily forward from the commencement to the completion of the same, a sufficient gang or gangs of men being always employed during the usual working hours.

No deviations to be made in any manner from the covenants and agreements in this specification, and, in case any work should not be to the satisfaction of the above-named J. G. Swindell, the same to be immediately altered and amended.

The care of the works rests with the contractor alone, the owner not being accountable for anything stolen, or for any loss or damage; and in case any unforeseen circumstance should take place, or any accident, of whatever kind, should arise, causing additional trouble,—workmanship, or making good such work,—is included in the contractor's accountability, and is to be rectified or made good by him without any extra or additional charge beyond the amount of the contract.

The contractor is to provide all labour, tools, tackle, buckets, windlasses, ropes, boring augers, and all and every tool or requisite for carrying on the works; the bricks, sand, cement, and pipes for lining the bore-hole being alone found by the employer.

In case the contractor shall delay the work or refuse to proceed with the same, the employer, after having given the contractor one week's notice in writing, is at liberty to take possession of all materials or tackle that are on the ground belonging to the contractor, and which he, the said contractor, forfeits by delay or refusal. The employer shall also be at liberty to engage other workman or workmen, and to deduct all the cost and charges thereof, from money due for previous work done by the contractor, the said contractor forfeiting by his delay or refusal all such money.

The amount of the contract-money to be paid by weekly instalments, calculated to reserve one-half of the cost of the works done, and subject to a certificate from the architect that they are going on to his satisfaction, and are sufficiently advanced to warrant such payments. The balance of the amount due to the contractor on the completion of the work to be paid within one week after the fixing of the permanent pumps.

Digging and Steining.—To excavate a well 4 feet diameter in the clear when the steining is finished, and of a depth of 200 feet; place the earth removed conveniently for wheeling away, the wheeling being performed by the employer. Stein in 4½-inch brickwork the said well; the bricks to be laid dry, with, at intervals, three courses set in cement, such intervals to be regulated by the nature of the clay, but in no case to exceed 5 feet apart; shut out all land-springs by bricking entirely in cement and puddling behind the same. Ten feet from the surface of the ground the steining to be 9-inch work, laid in cement, so as to block out surface drainage.   Pump or bale out any accumulated water that may occur during the progress of the work.   Fill up all putlog holes, and leave the steining in a perfect state.

Boring.—At the bottom of the said well, when it has attained the depth of 200 feet, insert, full 2 feet into the bottom, a cast-iron pipe, 12 inches diameter and 9 feet long; then bore with an 11½-inch auger, shell, or other tool requisite, and fit into the hole 8-inch wrought-iron boring pipes of the usual construction; after attaining a depth of bore at which the 8-inch pipes will no longer drive, insert 6-inch; make all joints in the said pipes secure and good, providing the solder and materials for the purpose.   The lower pipes to be well driven into the spring, and to have holes in the same to allow sufficient waterway; the upper pipe to stand 12 feet above the bottom of the shaft.   Provide and fix all temporary wooden trunks before commencing boring, and do all temporary work required during the progress of the boring and other work.

Contract.—I, ——, of ——, do hereby engage and agree with ——, of ——, for and in consideration of the sums undermentioned, to do all the labour, finding all tools and tackle necessary in digging, steining, and boring a well, to be done in strict and literal accordance with the covenants and directions of the foregoing specification.   The same to be done in the most workmanlike manner and to the entire satisfaction of Mr. J. G. Swindell, architect.   The contract-money to be as follows, viz. :—For executing completely the 200 feet of well-work ——; for the first 100 feet of boring at the rate of——; the next 20 feet an increase of——per foot, and increasing per foot every 20 feet deep the sum of ——. I hereby undertake to go on with the work till ordered in writing by my employer to stop, and to satisfactorily complete the work, without any extra charge beyond the said money mentioned above, which is to be calculated only to the depth of the work actually done.

N. B.—The reason no prices are given in the above is because so doing might greatly mislead, a variety of matters influencing the expense of the works in such uncertain operations as well-work: framing the contract so as only to pay for what is actually done is fairest both to the employer and contractor, and is therefore adopted in this contract. In the following work it was expected that water would be found about 85 to 90 feet from the surface; experience showed that 81 feet was the point where the spring was entered. Contracting, therefore, for 50 feet certain, and then at an increasing schedule of prices, was considered the best method of proceeding: here all things were found by the contractor.

Specification of certain works required to be done in sinking and steining a well for ———, of ———, to be excavated in a field called Great Daws, in a part of it to be pointed out to the contractor.

Excavator.—To excavate a well 4 feet diameter in the clear when finished and steined; to be sunk as deep as directed by Mr. Swindell, architect, under whose superintendence the work is to be done; provide all buckets, tackle, ropes, windlass, &c. necessary for removing the products of the excavation, which are to be placed or piled in a part of the field where directed, within 60 feet of the opening of the shaft; provide all shoring, boring augers necessary for feeling the work, as the excavation proceeds; remove all extraneous water, and do all things necessary for completing the works.

Steining.—The bricks to be new, sound, hard, square, well-burned gray stocks. The steining to be 4½-inch work, and to be laid dry in the most careful and approved manner, between the courses laid in cement, which cemented rings are to be three courses thick, and to occur as close as may be necessary for the stability of the work, never exceeding 5 feet apart. Where land-springs occur, or in bad ground, the steining to be executed entirely in cement, and puddled behind. The first 4 feet from the surface to be steined in 9-inch work set in cement. The best Roman cement and sharp Thames sand to be used; the former to be gauged with half sand.

The contract and conditions do not differ materially from those last given; and in both is a clause whereby the employer engages to pay the contractor, and to fulfil his part of the agreement, on receiving a satisfactory certificate from the architect that the works are going on well.

Some Remarks on the Wells for supplying the Fountains in Trafalgar Square.

From the position of the fountains, the discussions their appearance gave rise to, and the circumstances attending their execution, this national work is well worth attention : a descriptive sketch is therefore given of the wells, and of the engine for raising the water. The water is supplied by two wells, connected together by a tunnel, or driftway, which is run in the clay at a point lower than the position in the wells to where the water rises; the wells and tunnel are calculated to hold, when the water has attained its maximum height, 122,000 gallons. One of these wells is in Orange Street, and about 180 feet deep, with a diameter of 6 feet; the other is in front of the National Gallery, and is of very nearly the same depth, with a diameter of 4 feet 6 inches; the driftway is 6 feet diameter, and occurs about 5 feet from the bottom of the shafts; this driftway, or tunnel, is horizontal. The boring, which commenced at the bottom of the shaft, was continued to a greater depth in the well opposite the National Gallery than in the one in Orange Street; the total depth from the surface being, in one case, 395, while, in the other, it was about 300 feet. The use of the tunnel is almost self-evident; it acts, as may be supposed, as a reservoir to store the water while the engine is not at work; thus insuring a sufficiency to supply the pumps, even should they draw the water away from the well faster than the same is supplied by the spring. The strata passed through by the two wells may be thus stated upon the authority of a section published in the ' Illustrated London News.'

One in front of National Gallery.		One in Orange Street.	
Made ground	. . 9 feet	Made ground	. . 15 feet
Gravel.	. . . 5 „	Gravel.	. . . 5 „
Shifting sand	. . 7 „	Loam and gravel .	. 10 „
Gravel	. . . 2 „	London clay	. 145 „
London clay	. . 142 „	Thin layer of shells.	
Thin layer of shells.		Plastic clay .	. . 30 „
Plastic clay .	. . 30 „	Gravel and stones	. 10 „
Green-sand, pebbles, &c.	11 „	Green-sand .	. . 35 „
Green-sand .	. . 42 „		
Chalk .	. . . „		

Total depth to chalk is therefore 248 feet, and total depth of well and bore 395 feet.

Chalk, which, according to the above, is distant from the surface 250 feet, the bore being continued to a total depth from surface of ground of about 300 feet.

The pumping engines are on the Cornish plan; one is of the usual construction, having a beam, and the other, which is chiefly required as a reserve engine, is direct-acting, that is, the beam is dispensed with, and the piston-rod of the engine connected by rods directly on to the pumps. Though the mode of action of these and other Cornish engines cannot be thoroughly explained without complicated drawings, yet the following will give some idea of it, and, if attentively read over, while watching the working of an engine of this description, may assist the reader in the comprehension of its action. The steam, as before remarked in the Chapter on Pumps, &c., acts on the piston, if the engine be a beam engine, only during its down-stroke: to regulate this, a valve is required, situated so as to open and shut the communication between the steam in the boiler and the top of the cylinder, in which the piston slides, and a similar valve opening a communication between the top and the bottom of the cylinder: now, should this be open, the steam valve being shut, the piston will rise, for the counterweight at the opposite end of the beam will pull the piston upwards, and the steam will circulate from the top to the bottom of the cylinder. A third valve is also required to open and shut a communication between the bottom of the cylinder and the vessel in which the steam is condensed; so that the steam, which in the down-stroke of the piston caused its motion, is, after having changed its position, by the opening of the equilibrium valve, from the top to the bottom of the cylinder, then by the opening of the exhaust valve, let into the condenser. With this explanation the double stroke of the engine may be understood: supposing the steam valve and exhaust valve, opened by the preponderance of weights, released by the cataract, or instrument for regulating the distance between the strokes, a downward motion of the piston commences, when at about one-third of its stroke, or less, the motion of the engine shuts the steam valve, the exhaust valve remaining open, the expansion of the steam shut in the upper part of the cylinder causes the piston to continue its motion to near the bottom of the cylinder, and at a point a little above the end of the stroke the exhaust valve is shut. The engine is now quite stationary; at the proper period the cataract releases the equilibrium valve weight; the valve rises, and the up-stroke is performed by the aid of the counterweight, as before remarked. On the engine shutting the equilibrium valve, the up-stroke of the piston is stopped, and, after a definite period, by the action of the cataract, the steam valve is again opened. The steam being condensed, the under-side of the piston, it is almost needless to remark, is in vacuo during its down-stroke: this condensing apparatus is not common to the pumping engine alone, but is usually applied in all large engines. The advantage of condensation is equivalent to an increased pressure of steam in the boiler, for it is manifestly the same thing in effect to withdraw a certain resistance opposed to the motion of the piston as to add additional urging force, the resistance being retained; and if, further, this resistance can be removed with less expenditure than the increased pressure can be gained, it is clear its removal is more desirable than increasing the pressure of steam. To condense the exhaust steam, we require plenty of cold water; to increase the boiler pressure, we require more fuel, and circumstances will determine which of these two it will be best to expend.

Artesian Well lately sunk at Camden Station.

This work differs from the two former examples in the description of steam engine and arrangement of the pumps, for as the engine is required to do other work besides pumping, the ordinary pumping engine is inadmissible. The well, the pumps, and the motive power are therefore mentioned in order. Firstly, the well; this is sunk to a depth of 180 feet, of a diameter in the clear of 9 feet 6 inches, and the steining is executed throughout the entire depth in cement. For 28 feet from the surface, unusual precautions are taken to exclude landsprings, &c.; they are, first, an inner steining of half brickwork set in cement; next, segmental cylinders of iron; next, a thickness of about 9 inches of concrete; and lastly, behind all this, a 9-inch steining of brickwork. From the depth of 28 feet from the surface, the steining is 14 inches thick, and bonding curbs of iron occur at intervals. The boring, which commences at a depth of 180 feet from the surface, is continued for 220 feet, and is of a diameter of 12 inches. The water rises in the well 36 feet from the bottom, or to a height of 44 feet from the surface of the ground. The well-work was executed by Mr. Paten, of Watford; the pump-work and engines were made by Messrs. Bury, Curtis, and Kennedy, of Liverpool. The ground passed through in the execution of this well was as follows:

Section of the Well at Camden Station.

	Feet
Made ground	9
Loam and gravel	6
Black earth	3
Blue clay	144
Mottled clay	36
Green-sand	1
Pebbles	2
Mottled clay	8
Plastic clay	17
Loam and sand	5
Pebbles and sand	2
Carried forward . . .	233

					Feet.
Brought forward	.	.	.	.	233
Bed of flints .	.	.	.	.	1
Chalk .	.	.	.	.	166
Total depth	.	.	.	.	400

The boring-pipes are continued 60 feet up the well, the water being admitted from them by a sluice, which is situated about 4 feet from the bottom of the shaft. This sluice is worked by a handle placed above the water-level; the pipes themselves are steadied by stays, which are secured to the brickwork of the well.

Secondly; the pumps are in two pairs, each consisting of a lifting-pump for the lower, and a plunger-pump for the upper lift. This arrangement of four pumps is used to insure uniformity of motion, for the steam engine being double-acting, that is, giving out as much power during the up as the down stroke of the piston, requires an equal resistance for each stroke. The lifting-pumps empty their water into a wrought-iron cistern, which is about 4 feet deep and 3 feet 2 inches over, the back of it being curved to suit that of the well; the plan of the cistern being that of a sector. The suction-pipes of the plunger-pumps are inserted into this cistern; the plungers are 8 inches diameter, and the buckets of the lifting pumps, 8¾". The rising mains of the latter are 11 inches diameter; the mains of the plunger-pumps are of course smaller, the working parts of the pumps being outside, and not surrounded by the mains, as the lifting-buckets are. For the same reason, only one main is required for the plunger-pumps; at the bottom of this is situated an air vessel, which is an apparatus whereby a constantly uniform stream of water flows from the main; its construction is very simple. It may be described as a vessel larger than the rising main, and into which, through an air-tight opening at the upper end, the main dips so as nearly to touch the bottom of the vessel: water from the pumps being injected into this vessel will compress the air included in the space between the orifice of the main and the upper part of the vessel; the elasticity of this compressed air will therefore continue to drive the water which has risen above the orifice up the main during the interval that the pumps are stationary, which is at the period of the change of stroke.

Thirdly; the motive power for working the pumps consists of a high-pressure beam engine of the usual construction, which, as before remarked, performs other work as well as pumping. This engine is of 27 horse-power. The power required for raising the water can be determined by any one, as all the data are here given for the calculation, it being borne in mind that the cistern into which the water is forced is 40 feet above the surface of the ground. The steam engine has a 4-feet stroke, and the motion of the pumps being taken off the beam, at points respectively midway between the centre of the beam and the two ends, gives as the stroke of the pumps 2 feet. The speed at which the engine travelled when the author visited the works was twenty-one revolutions per minute. The duplicate boilers for this engine are of the Cornish description; they are 5 feet 10 inches diameter, and 22 feet long; sufficient steam is generated by one of them working singly, the other is kept as a reserve. The strength of the spring was tested when the works were completed, and the following was the result. The engine began to work at nine o'clock in the morning, and by continual pumping till twelve, lowered the water 11 feet 6 inches; by three o'clock, the engine still working, the water was lowered 6 inches more; at that point no further diminution was remarked. The water is remarkably soft, and for domestic purposes is excellent, but it does not answer for supplying the boilers of locomotive engines. Annexed is an analysis of the water of the well under considera-tion, as also of that drawn from the wells belonging to the Railway Company at the Watford and Tring Stations: all these are sunk in the chalk formation, yet a great difference exists in the constituents of the impurities of the water. The analysis in all cases was made by R. Phillips, Esq.

Situation.	Sulphate Soda.	Carbonate Soda.	Muriate Soda.	Carbonaceous Matter and Trace of Silica.	Sulphate Lime.	Carbonate Lime.	Total Solid Matter.
							Grains.
Camden .	13·00	17·60	11·10	2·30	..	..	44·00
Watford .	..	..	1·90	1·32	·94	19·54	23·70
Tring . .	..	..	1·38	1·61	1·09	14·72	18·80

The quantity of water experimented upon in the above analysis was one gallon in each case. The above particulars of the Camden well were obtained by the kindness of R. B. Dockray, Esq., C. E., through the means of documents in the Engineer's office, Euston Station, and from personal examination of the pump-work, &c. in the well itself.

Well at the Hanwell Lunatic Asylum.

This work, which was executed a few years since, is remarkable on account of the height to which the water rises; indeed, the district is well suited for a purely Artesian well, and in this case it is quite evident that, had the well been entirely bored, the same amount of water would have been obtained, deducting the retarding action caused by the friction of the water against the sides of the bore-pipe. In the 'Sixty-eighth Report of the Visiting Justices of the County Lunatic Asylum at Hanwell' is a notice of this well, from which the following is compiled. The section of the ground passed through is as follows :

Section of the Well at Hanwell.

	Feet.	Inches.
Vegetable soil, sand, and gravel . . .	20	0
Blue clay, with some brick clay on the top, and veins of stone occurring at intervals .	168	0
Indurated mud and sand	22	0
Carried forward . .	210	0

D

		Feet.	Inches.
Brought forward . . .		210	0
Pebbles and shells		2	0
Mottled clay		23	0
Sand and water		2	0
Mottled clay		13	0
Indurated sand and mud		9	0
Clay		8	0
Green-sand and clay		8	0
Bed of hard oyster-shells		3	6
Pebbles		3	6
Flint stones bored into		8	0
Total depth		290	0

In sinking this well, the shaft was carried down for the first 30 feet of a diameter of 10 feet; from that point the diameter was 6 feet to that part of the mottled clay in which the iron cylinders were affixed. The cylinders were then lined with a brick steining, and the boring was continued from thence to the bed of flints in which the work was discontinued. The supply of water from the sand-spring rose to within 16 feet of the surface of the ground; from the pebbles overlying the flints, the water rose to a further height of 8 feet, and from the bed of saturated flint stones, the water rose so as to overflow the surface at the rate of 100 gallons per minute; and, 26 feet above the surface, the water overflowed at the rate of 23 gallons per minute. The supply proving so great, the large diameter of the first 30 feet of well was found useless, and a rising main of iron was fitted to a cap which was inserted at that part of it where the 6-feet diameter commenced. The temperature of the water is about 55° Fahrenheit, and contains in each gallon 48 grains of solid matter, consisting of salts of lime and soda, with a trace of iron.

Messrs. Verey's Well, Kilburn.

This work was executed under the superintendence of the late Mr. J. G. Swindell about the year 1848: the diameter in the clear for 250 feet in depth is 4 feet; after that, boring

commences, and is carried down to the sand-spring of a diameter of 8 inches, and to a total depth from the surface of
about 280 feet. The rise of water is to about 150 feet, or
rather less, from the surface. The original intention in sinking
this well was to have bored after attaining a depth of 200 feet
(the water-level being well known in this district); but had
such intention been persevered in, fears were entertained that
the 50 feet of water in the well, being only the upper head of
the spring, would be insufficient to supply the wants of the
brewery: the extra 50 feet of digging were therefore ultimately
determined on, and the experiment detailed in the following
pages proves the view taken to have been correct; for if pumps
be fixed at too high a level above the spring, the hydrostatic
pressure of water is insufficient to cause the water to rise in
the well fast enough to supply the pumps, even should they
be small ones. The works were commenced in April, 1848, and
for the first 10 feet the brickwork was in cement 9 inches thick,
to exclude land-springs from the well: about 25 feet were executed the first week, and after that the work averaged about
20 feet to the week, some weeks a little more, some a little
less; the stiffness of the clay and the claystones, or septaria,
which were found at intervals, affecting the speed of the work.
The London or blue clay, which was soon arrived at, extended
to a depth of 235 feet,—the mottled clay, pebbles and sand
followed much in the order of the sections before given,—
while in the mottled clay the steining was not left unsupported
with such impunity as in the blue clay: it is of a more soapy
or slimy nature, and exposure to the air, together with these
properties, renders it more likely to allow the brickwork to slip.
On the execution of the steining it is only necessary to remark
that the work was laid partly in cement and partly dry, and
of a thickness of 4½ inches. The cement used was blue lias
(Greaves's patent), and the bricks partly stocks and partly
malm paviours. The cement was used stale and mixed thin,
since otherwise it would have become partially set in being conveyed down the shaft to the workmen, as, when near the full

depth, the time of journey down the well was nearly of three minutes' duration.* The boring pipes were of wrought iron, the lower lengths perforated, the junctions being tinned in the usual manner. On obtaining the water, the quantity was tested by the aid of a temporary pump, the application of which is also useful in clearing the work, and ascertaining if any sand has blown into the well: this pump was an ordinary lifting pump of 6 inches diameter, and working with a stroke in the barrel of about 9 inches; the rising main was bolted directly over the pump-barrel, which by it was thus suspended in the water; the main, on its passage up the well, was steadied by timbers; the rods worked by this arrangement in the rising main, and were carried to the top of the well, where motion was given to them by eight men: the result of the experiment was, that the pump, which threw about 24 gallons per minute, lowered the water about 33 feet, but no further, thus proving the strength of the spring when a head of 33 feet of water was taken off. Here the advantage of drawing the water from a point under its surface, as far as practicable, is made manifest; indeed, the question is one turning on a law of hydrostatics, well known and easily calculated. The pumps were executed by another party, and it may suffice to say that they are of the description technically called three-throw pumps, and very good of their kind. The cost of executing this well, exclusive of the pumpwork, both temporary and permanent, was about £200.

---

* The manner of using cement described in the text is one so contradictory to all the laws affecting that class of materials, that it is not possible to protest against it too strongly. In such a case as this, if it had been necessary to mix the mortar, or cement, above-ground, the proper material to have been employed would have been blue lias *lime*, or some hydraulic lime whose rate of setting would have been sufficiently slow. Mortar made with an excess of water loses nearly all its valuable qualities; when used stale it is also inferior to that which is fresh; and the same remarks apply, with even greater importance, to every description of cement.—G. R. B.

Well at Hampstead Heath, belonging to the Hampstead Water Company.

This well was sunk in the year 1833, down to the main sand-spring, a depth of about 320 feet, and of a diameter of seven feet. Subsequently, as a rather greater supply of water was desired, a bore was carried into the chalk. The steining of the well is 9-inch work, laid dry, between rings set in cement; the back steining has its cement rings midway between those of the front steining. The lower part of the steining is held up by four tie-rods, which are bolted to a cast-iron curb let into the brickwork some distance up the shaft. The section of the ground passed through during the two operations of digging and boring is given below. The situation is on the lower Heath, where the Bagshot sands are wanting.

	Feet.
Yellow clay	30
Blue clay	259
Plastic clay	40
Sand	49
Bed of flints, very thin, chalk hard . .	40
Do. soft, with water . . .	4
Chalk hard, no water	28

From this section it will be seen, that after passing the chalk spring, the hard chalk underlying it supplied no water, thus proving that in sinking wells in this formation, when it is very hard, no water can be expected, till long lines of flints, fissures, or softer chalk, are arrived at. Mr. Hakewell, the Engineer under whose orders this boring was executed, paid particular attention to the conditions of the supply from the chalk, and the fact that no water was furnished by the hard bed under the spring influenced his proceedings in the execution of the well at Kentish Town. The water is raised in this well by means of three lifting pumps, situated at different heights up the shaft. Each lift averages about 100 feet, and the sizes of the pumps are $8\frac{3}{4}''$ diameter of bucket, by a length of stroke of 2 feet 3 inches; the lowest pump is slung in the water by having its rising main, which is of larger diameter than the bucket, secured by flanches and bolts to cast-iron girders, arranged for that purpose in the well, where the two lower lifts terminate. The pump-rods pass through stuffing-boxes from inside the rising main. The cisterns, from which the second lift draws from the first, and the third from the second, are very small, being only branched from the rising main, and in capacity but little larger in diameter than the pump-barrel, just in fact sufficient to hold a supply for the higher lift. The rods, when inside the mains, are steadied by triangular guiding pieces encircling them, and, where outside the mains, they pass through wooden cleats, which are secured to cast-iron girders. Situated at the top of the well is a cast-iron framing, with upright guides. Between these guides work cast-iron wheels; to the axle of these wheels the pump-rods, and also the connecting rods from the cranks, are attached; thus, though the tendency of the crank in its revolution is to pull the rods from a vertical line, the effect of the pulleys is to keep their motion in a straight one.

Some important observations may be made upon the results of the wells described above, all of which are sunk in what is called the London Basin. Firstly, In the case of the Camden Town well, the quality of the waters is such as to show that the whole supply is furnished by the loam and sands of the basement beds of the London clay. The boring in the chalk, under these circumstances, was worse than useless, for it only let the water from the sands into a part of the subjacent formation, which was likely to be more absorbent than the surface, because at the junction of any two strata there usually exists a layer of silt or clay which renders the escape of water from the upper to the lower rather difficult. This well may be considered as having been carried down 166 feet deeper than was necessary.

Secondly, In the chalk itself there does not appear to be any other indication of the flow of water sufficient to guide the operations of the Engineer, than what is furnished by the

materials traversed. The water circulates through it principally along the lines of fissures, and not by general permeation
of the whole mass, owing to its general porous nature and its
close texture. It happens, however, especially when it under-
lies some impervious stratum, that the body of the chalk itself
is saturated with water, and a portion is left free to circulate
upon any retentive layer which may exist within it. The
layers of flint, which sometimes occur in regular stratification
over large areas, serve to hold up this free portion in the
upper or soft chalk; and it therefore must be upon the top of
these layers that we must seek for a supply to a well sunk in
this formation, unless any water-bearing fissure be traversed.
In the lower members of the series, the comparatively speaking impervious beds of the chalk marl perform the same
function of water-bearing strata that the beds of flint do in the
wells hitherto sunk near London.

The very remarkable work, by Mr. J. Prestwich, upon the
'Water-bearing Strata of London,' should be in the hands of
every person who desires to become acquainted with this
branch of Engineering.

Well at Fort Regent, Jersey.

This work has been described by Major H. D. Jones, R.E.,
in the 'Professional Papers of the Corps of Royal Engineers.'
The following quotation from parts of his description will
no doubt be acceptable to the reader:—"Fort Regent was
constructed during the late war between Great Britain and
France. The works were commenced about the year 1806.
The fort is erected upon the Town Hill, a bold promontory to
the south of the town of St. Helier, which it commands most
completely, the town being built at the foot of the rock. The
summit of the hill was above 170 feet above the level of high
water. In its character it very much resembles Gibraltar, a
bold rocky feature, rising abruptly from the sea, and having
scarcely any perceptible connexion with the hills to the north-
ward and eastward, which encircle the town in those directions.

The South Hill is formed of compact syenite, weighing 165 lbs. per cubic foot. The rock is stratiform, with vertical joints; the general direction is east and west. There were no springs upon the surface of the hill, nor anything indicating on the face of the scarped rock that it contained such an abundant supply of water; it must, consequently, have been upon the conviction that water would be found by sinking to the same level as the water stood at the Pigeon Pump, in Hill Street, (240 yards distant from the point where the well in the fort has been sunk,) that Major Humphry, the commanding Engineer, was induced to recommend the attempt being made. The operation, although it cost much time, labour, and expense, has been most completely successful. After sinking through 234 feet of compact rock, and upon firing a blast, the spring was laid open, the water from which immediately rose in the shaft to a height of 70 feet, and has rarely since been lower. During the progress of the work, water had been found at different points, but not in any quantity sufficient to retard the workmen, until the lucky blast above mentioned, when it poured in like a torrent, to the great astonishment of the miners who were suspended in the bucket, waiting the effects of the explosion." The temperature of the water in this well is 50° Fahrenheit. Some further memoranda from the same source are:—"The following details, extracted from the office books, will afford some idea of the difficulty of the operation, and the time and labour consumed in sinking the well. The work was commenced in December, 1806, and continued night and day until November, 1808:

Commenced 1806.	Number of Miners per month.	Feet sunk per month.	Price paid per foot.
December . . .	14	13	Livres. 60
1807.			
January . . .	12	8½	72
February . . .	12	3	96
March . . .	12	9	108
April	—	—	—
May	12 .	5	120
June	12	11	108
July	12	8½	108
August . . .	12	10¼	111
September . . .	12	10	108
October . . .	12	9¼	108
November . . :	12	9	108
December . . .	12	9	108
1808.			
January . . .	12	9½	108
February . . .	12	7½	108
March . . .	12	10¾	108
April	12	9	108
May	12	12¼	108
June	12	13	108
July	12	10	108
August . . .	12	11¾	108
September . . .	12	9¼	108
October . . .	12	9	108

Average cost, 10s. per foot.—Total expense, £ 2599. 8s. 7½d.

" There were expended, during the progress of the work, of the following articles, the under-mentioned quantities, viz. :

Candles	976 lbs.
Coals	1659 bushels.
Gunpowder	2848 lbs.
Lamp oil	82 gallons.
Miners' tubes	9852.

" There are two cisterns capable of holding 8000 gallons each. The water is pumped into them by machinery, to be worked either by horses or men, the same machinery being applicable to the working of a bucket in case the pump should be out of order. The pump is 4 inches diameter, with brass bucket and valves, with 195 feet of wrought-iron rod, jointed every ten feet, and eighteen 10-feet lengths of 5½-inch iron pipe.   Cost, £495. 15s.

"The machinery for working a bucket from the horse-wheel, independent of the pump, consisting of a barrel on the horizontal shaft, with clutch-box, lever, and pulleys for leading the ropes, cost about £35."—"The total expense, including the labour in fixing machinery or incidental expenses, amounted to £667. 15s. Thus, for a sum little exceeding £3000, there is obtained for the garrison an inexhaustible supply of excellent water. Twenty-four men, working for two hours, without fatiguing themselves, can with ease pump into the cisterns 800 gallons of water."

Artesian Well at Grenelle.

This well was sunk at the expense of the town of Paris, for the purpose of supplying the abattoir, and the district or quarter of Grenelle, under the directions of M. Mulot.

At St. Ouen and St. Denis, near Paris, Artesian wells had already been sunk through the tertiary formations, until they reached the sands which lie upon the chalk; and a copious supply had been obtained from them.   But at Grenelle it was known that so great a difference existed in the geological structure of these formations, that it became necessary to resort to some other source.   The 'calcaire grossier,' in fact, of the more northerly parts of Paris is replaced at Grenelle by a series of marls and clays, which do not allow the free passage of the subterranean sheet of water.   M. Mulot, then, reasoning upon the results obtained by the wells at Elbœuf and Rouen, considered that it would be necessary to traverse the chalk formation itself, and to obtain a supply from the lower green-sands.   At Elbœuf, where the ground is about 27 feet above the sea, the water rose to about 82 feet above the ground, or 109 feet above the sea.   As the plain of Grenelle is 104 feet above that level, M. Mulot thought, very correctly, that if he reached the same sheet, the water would necessarily flow over the surface. MM. Arago and Walferdin, who brought to M. Mulot's assistance the influence of their scientific knowledge and their great reputation, found in the course of their examination of the district that the level of the green-sands at Lusigny, 12 miles above Troyes, where the Seine leaves those formations, was nearly 300 feet above that of the plain of Grenelle. The inference they drew from this fact was, that the water would not only overflow the bore-hole, but also rise to a very considerable height above the ground.

Upon these reasonings M. Mulot commenced his work; and after eight years of indefatigable labour, in spite of all the accidents of the undertaking and the sneers of the incredulous, on the 26th of February, 1841, his perseverance was crowned with the most signal success. The depth attained at the period of reaching water was not less than 1802 feet from the surface, or about 1698 feet below the level of the sea. The strata traversed were as follows:

Drift gravel, about	33 ft.	0 in.
Sand, clays, lignites, &c., replacing the cal-caire grossier	100	0
Fragments of chalk in a species of clay .	16	6
Chalk	1378	0
Chalk marl	88	6
Gault clay and green-sands . . .	186	0
Total	1802	0

When the water rose to the surface, it was ascertained to be of a temperature of 81°·81 Fahrenheit; and it remains of that degree to the present day. M. Walferdin, who watched the progress of the work with great interest, made a series of observations to ascertain the law of increase of temperature at great depths. He found that at Paris the thermometer remained constantly at 53°·06 Fahrenheit in the cellars of the Observatory, which are 94 feet below the surface: in the chalk, at 1319 feet from the surface, it marked 76°·3; in the gault, at 1657 feet, it marked 79°·61; thus showing that in the depth of 1553 feet the increase of temperature was 26°·55, or about 1°·7 Fahrenheit for every succeeding hundred feet beyond the depth of constant temperature. According to this law, the temperature at the depth of 1802 feet from the surface ought to have been 81°·96 nearly; and that of the waters, stated above to be 81°·81, is a striking illustration of the beauty and correctness of the inductive reasoning followed by M. Walferdin.

Amongst the numerous difficulties attending a work of this kind, those arising from the rupture or fall of the boring-tools were the most dangerous. Thus, when a depth of 1250 feet had been reached, a length of about 270 feet of the rods fell to the bottom, and broke into several pieces. It required all the ingenuity of M. Mulot, and not less than 15 months' labour, to remove the fragments, one by one, by the aid of a screw-tap, which was made to fit upon the ends of the rods. In April, 1840, a chisel fell to the bottom, and buried itself in the solid chalk. In this case it became necessary to clear away all round the tool, and to raise it by the same means as before. About three months before the water-bearing stratum was reached, a shell also fell to the bottom: M. Mulot pushed this aside, and continued the boring beyond it.

Drawings of some of the tools used by M. Mulot are added.

a.   *b.*   *c.*

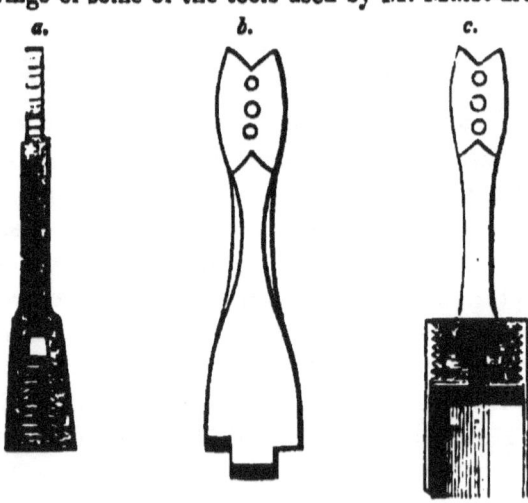

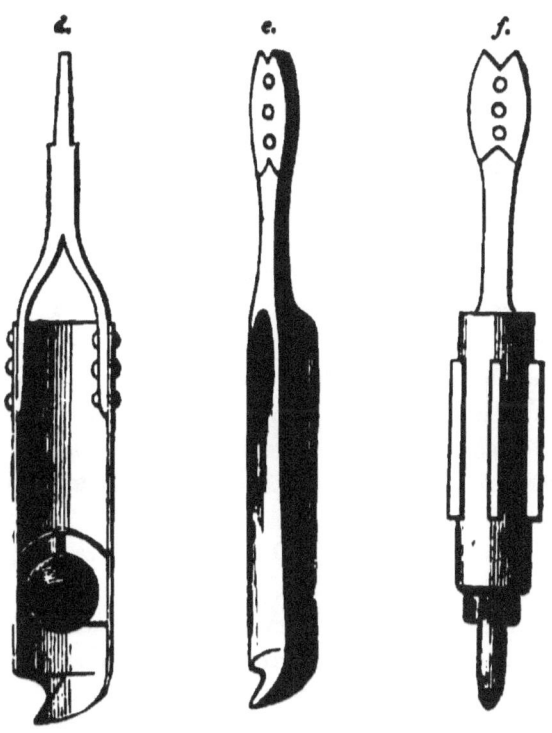

a, is the screw-tap contrived for raising the fragments of the rods from the bore.

b, a chisel, similar to the one which fell to the bottom.

c, a screwed plug, fitting into the tubes, by which these are lowered to their positions.

d, a scoop, with ball-clack, for removing wet sand.

e, an ordinary shell.

f, an auger for enlarging the bore to place tubes.

The quantity of water supplied by this well is about 800,000 gallons per day, rising to a height of 122 feet above the ground. The total cost was about 400,000 francs. It is to be observed that even now the rising pipes are occasionally choked with the sand from below.

Artesian Wells in the Valley of the Loire, near Tours.

M. Degousée mentions that he has executed no less than sixteen borings of this description in the department of the Indre et Loire, of which ten are in Tours itself, and six in the neighbourhood; their average depth is about 150 mètres, or 500 feet. Only two of these borings were unsuccessful, viz., that of Ferrières Larçon, and that of Evres, situated in the neighbourhood of the outcrop of the cretaceous formations, upon the Jurassic limestone of the province of the Poitou. All the others furnish a copious supply, and, with the exception of that of Marmontier, the water flows over the surface. The waters of these wells are employed for many industrial purposes, amongst which the most interesting are their adaptation to mills and irrigation. The cost of these wells was upon the average about £1 per foot lineal of descent.

The well at the abattoir of Tours passes through the lower tertiary formations and the alluvions of the Valley of the Loire. The water rises from the green-sands, below the chalk, which immediately succeeds the tertiaries; and the total depth of the boring is 146 mètres, or about 478 feet. M. Degousée mentions that subsequently to the execution of this boring uuder his orders, M. Mulot executed another at the hospital in the immediate vicinity, and that the yield of the well of the abattoir has been considerably diminished in consequence.

The non-success of the borings at Evres and Ferrières is worthy of remark, as illustrating the uncertainty of this class of operations. At Evres, the chalk is covered by 395 feet of marls, sands, and sandstones of the tertiary formations, yielding water. The chalk is about 167 feet thick, and the clays and sands of the subcretaceous series are traversed to a depth of 66 feet without any water rising from them. The total depth of this well is exactly 191·66 mètres, or 628 feet 6 inches. At Ferrières, the chalk was met with at 30 feet from the surface, and traversed in a thickness of 219 feet.

The boring was continued to an additional depth of 235 feet, or about 454 feet from the surface in the clays and sands of the subcretaceous formations, and was continued about 30 feet deeper in the marls of the Jura limestone series. As both these positions are favourably placed with respect to the level of the river Creuse, which is supposed to feed the Artesian wells in the Touraine, the only explanation of their unsuccess must be found in the existence of some fault by which the flow of the subterranean sheet of water is intercepted.

Well near Calais (Department of the Pas du Calais).

This well is another instance of the uncertain results to be met with in the prosecution of deep borings. The bore was continued through the chalk, and the whole range of the sub-cretaceous formations, into the transition rocks immediately underlying the green-sands ; but no water was met with,—under serviceable conditions at least. Mr. Prestwich gives the thickness of the strata traversed as follows:

	Feet.
Gravel, and loose wet sand	80
Clays, sand, and pebble beds	161
Chalk	762
Upper green-sand	3
Gault	24
Lower green-sand	17
Transition rocks	103
Total	1150

In this case, also, the subterranean stream is in all probability intercepted by a fault.

Well at Chichester.

In Mr. Gatehouse's Well, South Street, Chichester, the following strata were traversed:

Strata.	Thickness of strata.	From ground.
Vegetable mould . .	6 ft. 0 in.	
Gravel	16 6	22 ft. 6 in.

Strata.	Thickness of strata.	From ground.
. Red sand	0 ft. 6 in.	23 ft. 0 in.
Blue clays	60 0	83 0
Coloured (mottled) clays .	97 0	180 0
Chalk.	729 0	909 0
Chalk marl	61 0	970 0
Upper green-sand . .	84 0	1054 0

The boring was stopped in October, 1844, and about 370 feet in length of the rod, and the slush-pipe attached to it, were left in the bore; nor has any subsequent attempt been made to extract them. No pipes were used in the sand.

The quantity of water yielded is very small. One of the most remarkable facts connected with this well is, that the water-line is about 18 feet from the surface of the ground, whilst that of the wells of the same district, supplied by infiltration from the superficial gravel, is only six feet below the surface. The point where the Arun leaves the green-sand formation, a little above Chichester, is, however, at a sufficient elevation to have warranted the expectation that the water would have overflowed.

The water from this well at present is decidedly chalybeate, and has a very strong and repulsive taste and smell of sulphuretted hydrogen; its temperature is not such as to indicate that it rises from the green-sand.

Well at Southampton, on the Common.

This well was commenced upon a report made by Mr. Clark, of Tottenham, to the effect that a copious supply of water would be obtained from the chalk in the position of an experimental boring made by that contractor. The Town Council very unfairly, and, as circumstances proved, very unwisely, did not employ Mr. Clark to carry out the plan he suggested, but entered into a contract with a party in the town, who, as might have been anticipated, failed, and left the work to be completed by his sureties. The latter carried a well through the sands, clays, and mottled clays of the Hampshire tertiaries, into the chalk, to a depth of 560 feet from the surface of the ground, and about 106 feet into the chalk; a boring was then commenced, and after a period of fifteen years from the date of obtaining the Act of Parliament for these works, and a positive expense to the rate-payers of about £13,000, the work has lately been abandoned when a depth of not less than 1317 feet had been attained. As a question of abstract science this is to be regretted; because the solution of the question of the possibility of obtaining a supply by means of Artesian wells from below the chalk is very desirable, and it might be attained in this case with comparative ease. But the arguments brought forward by Mr. Ranger appear to be sufficiently cogent to justify the discontinuance of the experiment at the expense of the town. Public money should never be expended, in fact, unless with a certainty of attaining the end proposed; it should never be employed in carrying out theoretical views or for the attainment of what may be called hypothetical, or eventual, advantages. It is to be hoped that some scientific body, or some lovers of science, may take up this question in its present state.

The strata traversed may be briefly described as consisting of the following materials, viz.:

A series of sands and clays, with beds of loam, intercalated, which appear to represent the Bagshot sand formations of the London basin; in thickness	90 ft.	0 in.
Clay with lignite, shell limestone, pebbles, and sand of the tertiary formations . . .	261	6
Mottled clays and sands; the basement beds of the tertiaries	82	6
Chalk, with flints	851	0
Chalk marl, as far as boring has proceeded .	12	3

These dimensions, however, are only approximations, because it is almost impossible to say that the precise limits of either the great tertiary clay, or of the chalk marl, can be clearly defined.

Recent analysis of the water of this well shows that there is present in it a very large proportion of common salt in solution. If this be found to be the normal condition, it would lead to the conclusion that there is an under-ground communication with the sea, although the height to which the water rises (viz. 100 feet above the latter) proves that it can only exist by infiltration through the pores of the chalk.

Artesian Well at Northam, near Southampton.

In the lower part of the town of Southampton there are four wells, supplied by the waters rising from the lower members of the tertiary series. Two of these are in the Docks, one in the Railway Station, and one at Northam was sunk by the Town for the supply of the inhabitants.

The wells of the Docks and of the Railway Station vary from 220 to about 240 feet, and being very close together, they have produced a re-action, which has materially affected the quantity they respectively yield. The Northam well, however, is much deeper; for the bottom, still in the blue clay, is at 375 feet 6 inches from the surface, although the Dock and Railway wells derive their supplies apparently from the sands lying between the clay and the chalk. It would be fair to assume from this fact of the difference in the thickness of the strata, that the Northam well is situated upon a species of gully or depression of the chalk.

CHAPTER VIII.

STRATA OF ENGLAND AND WALES IN REFERENCE TO THEIR SPRINGS.

THE most superficial observer must be aware that the components of the surface of the earth vary greatly in different situations; in some places hard, crystalline, unstratified rocks

make their appearance; whilst in others soft strata, evidently bearing the character of having been deposited in
layers; will be found. This disposition a little closer examination will show not to be the result of an accidental con-
fusion, but to follow from an order of superposition which
it has been the province of Geology to ascertain. The purport
of the present chapter is to lay before the reader the relation
of these various substances composing the earth's crust, as
connected with the subject of springs; and because the surface of the crust may be taken as an index of what may be
expected underneath, it is desirable to give the order in which
the various rocks and deposits are found. The reason that
in all cases the same distance does not intervene between the
lower rocks and the earth's surface is simply from the fact of
the inclined, and not horizontal, position of the strata; and
the alteration in the position of the strata may easily be
traced to disturbances of a subsequent date to their deposition.
Although the lower rocks outcrop and show themselves in
many places on the earth's surface; and further, though some
usually intervening rocks may be, and often are, missing
between some of the upper and under beds of the series, yet,
except under very unusual circumstances, none of the upper
ones will underlie the deposit or rock which the order of superposition usually places them above. Descending from what
Geologists consider the latest formation, a section of the earth's
crust may be represented as follows; a great many subdivisions
being of course omitted.

Formations above the Chalk.

Vegetable soil, gravel, crag sand, London clay, septaria.
Plastic clay, with beds of sand.

Cretaceous Group.—Chalk, chalk marl, upper green-sand,
gault clay, lower green-sand, weald clay, iron sand.

Oolitic System, Upper Series.—Purbeck beds, Portland beds,
calcareous sand, Kimmeridge clay.

Middle Series.—Coral rag, yellow sands, calcareous-silicious
grits, Oxford clay.

Lower Oolitic Series.—Cornbrash limestone, and forest marble, great oolite, or softish freestone, layers of clay, Stonesfield slate, fullers' earth, clay, sandy limestone, or inferior oolite.

Lias Formation—which consists of limestone beds, divided by layers of clay.

New Red Sandstone Group—consisting of variegated marls, sandstones, conglomerates, gypsum, rock salt, bone red, or dark-coloured limestone, blue and blackish limestone, alternating with clay and marl, &c.

Magnesian limestone.

Carboniferous Group.—Coal measures, sandstones, clays, shales, ironstone, millstone grit, mountain limestone.

Old Red Sandstone Formation.

Silurian System, comprising argillaceous limestones, sandstones, quartzose flints, flagstones, schist.

Cambrian System, or inferior stratified rocks of clay slate—mica slate, with dark-coloured limestones, sandstones, &c.

Plutonic Rocks, as granite, syenite greenstone, hornblende, serpentine, &c.

It is not here intended to explain the properties of the various substances mentioned above, excepting so far as they are connected with the consideration of springs in them. The vegetable soil comes first under review ; such soil, if it rest on gravel or sand, will always be dry ; but if it rest on clay, or any other retentive strata, will, unless well drained, be a complete swamp ; on such a substratum rest those soils where the springs are within a few feet of the surface ; should, however, gravel or sand succeed the surface soil, no water can be expected in it till a retentive seam of clay or other impermeable matter be met with. When sand, as at Hampstead, rests on London clay, very little difficulty is occasioned in getting a sufficient water supply from it ; but such land-springs are, from their nature, very variable.

Gravel oftentimes rests on porous chalk, in many parts of Hertfordshire, for instance ; in such positions no water can be expected to be met with in wells in the gravel, but they must be sunk to the saturated point of the chalk.

London Clay.—In this formation there are few springs, and though by chance one may be met with, nobody would think of sinking a well in the London clay in full anticipation of getting water till that formation was passed through, and the beds of sand in the plastic clay formation were entered; in these there is a very copious supply.

Cretaceous Group.—The quantity of water in this group is enormous; the lower portion of the chalk itself, as far as the denseness of the material will allow, is fully saturated; all fissures in it are completely full, forming literally subterranean rivers. The strata directly under the chalk, consisting of retentive marl, will make it appear clear to all why the lower portions of this formation should contain so much water. The long lines of flint in chalk have been remarked on before, as favouring the percolation of water, and so has the fact that, in the London chalk basin, those circumstances exist that are required to insure the success of sinking Artesian wells. When wells are sunk in the lower green-sand formation, water may be met with where clay seams occur; the water which supplies the deep-seated springs is held up by the weald clay under the sand. The water supplied by the iron sand is generally arrived at by sinking deep wells; but it is often impregnated with iron.

In the upper oolite system little water can be expected in the impermeable beds of Purbeck and Portland stone, except in fissures; under the Portland bed, however, is porous matter, and the water absorbed by it is retained by the underlying clay, thus rendering it accessible. In the middle oolitic series, the Oxford or clunch clay is the retentive medium, and wells must be sunk to the saturated portions of the overlying porous matter. In the Oxford clay itself are few springs. The lower oolitic formation has water retained by clay seams. In the cornbrash limestone and forest marble the wells are not very deep; under the great oolite, the fullers' earth clay retains the water. The limestone itself is porous to a certain extent, therefore wells must be sunk in it to its line of saturation, or its junction with the clay underneath.

The upper retentive beds of the lias formation supply water to the wells sunk in the lower oolite; and water may be met with in the upper portions of the lias formation for the same reason. Wells sunk in the lower portions of the lias formation have water retained in them by the upper marls of the new red sandstone group.

The alternations of sandstone and clay, rock salt, &c. in the new red sandstone, render water procurable in that group. The newspaper accounts of a shaft sunk in this formation at Gorton, by the Manchester and Salford Water-works Company, relate that the well is seventy yards deep; there are radiating galleries from the main shaft, and the quantity of water raised by the engine equals 2,000,000 of gallons per day.

In the magnesian limestone, fissures and holes containing water must be worked for. The great quantity of water in the carboniferous group is probably known to all, it being an element which, were it not for the large pumping engines constantly at work, would greatly impede the operations of the miner: the alternating porous and retentive matter in this formation fully accounts for the appearance of the water. The mountain limestone being porous, water can only be met with when beds of clay occur; the lower portions, however, of this formation are saturated, because impervious layers separate it from the porous beds of the old red sandstone. In this latter formation there is no lack of water, its components being partly porous, with retentive intervening layers.

Owing to the stratified character of the Silurian system, water may be met with in it; and in the lower Plutonic rocks, where they show themselves at the surface, the only chance of getting water is by sinking till a fissure fully charged with water is arrived at. Such an operation as this was carried on at Fort Regent, before alluded to; the rock in which that well is sunk is compact syenite, intersected with vertical fissures.

The following remarks on the properties of water may be interesting to those who, having sunk a well, wish to ascertain the character of the water, or to others who may be called upon to approve or disapprove of any particular supply.

Perfectly pure water is never met with in nature; indeed, the addition of foreign matters renders it beneficial for a variety of purposes; should it be required, however, absolutely pure, recourse must be had to distillation. Its components by weight are eight parts of oxygen gas and one of hydrogen, making an aggregate of nine parts of pure water, which is quite tasteless, odourless, and colourless, is a great solvent, and absorber of gases; of some of them it absorbs its own bulk, which is one great reason why potable water should be kept free from the influence of all deleterious vapours and gases. Rain and snow water, when first collected, are considered as the purest water naturally supplied; to insure purity, they should be collected at some distance from any large town. This description of water is, however, peculiarly liable to the decomposition of the animal and vegetable matters it collects in its passage through the atmosphere. In hot weather and in hot climates, this change takes place most rapidly. Spring water is modified by the strata through which it traverses, and the expressions hardness and softness refer to the relative quantity of salts with which the same is charged. The earthy impurities have the property of decomposing soap, which substance, therefore, is a criterion to judge of the softness of any water. By adding to a given quantity of any water a certain amount of soap dissolved in alcohol, the appearance of the curdy precipitate formed will at once show the relative hardness of the liquid.

Some of the substances that are usually found in spring water are as under:

First, carbonic acid gas. The limits in which this gas

occurs vary of course with the chances the water has of absorbing it. When freely exposed, water will absorb as much as its own bulk. It may be detected by lime water, with which it forms a white insoluble precipitate.

Sulphuretted hydrogen gas is often found in mineral water. It may be detected by carbonate of lead, on the addition of which, when the gas is present, a dark tint will show itself.

Chloride of sodium, or common salt, is also an ingredient of some waters. This, together with muriatic acid, can be detected by the nitrate of silver. The precipitate thrown down, on exposure to light, soon turns black.

Carbonate of lime, or chalk, being insoluble, is never found in water; but when an excess of carbonic acid is present, the bicarbonate resulting is soluble, and is very commonly met with. Boiling some of the water will drive off the excess of carbonic acid, and the chalk will at once make its appearance in a thick cloud. It is this which occasions the fur on tea-kettles and boilers, where this description of water is used. Salts of lime are readily detected by oxalate of ammonia; also, when the quantity is great, by adding carbonate of soda. Ferro-prussiate of potash will make known the presence of salts of iron; and with salts of lead the metal will be precipitated slowly by a piece of zinc, or form a white precipitate with sulphuric acid. Nitrate of barytes will detect sulphuric acid. Salts of potash may be found by bichloride of platinum, which will form a yellow crystalline powder. Soda, which has properties similar to potash, differs from it in not forming a precipitate with the above-mentioned test.

According to the quantity and nature of the foreign matters found in water, so has it received certain names indicative of its character. Thus, saline waters are those that contain salts of soda, lime, or magnesia, &c., the combination generally being with sulphuric and muriatic acid. Chalybeate waters usually contain either carbonate or sulphate of iron. Many such springs of water are found; Tunbridge Wells, for instance. Sometimes the chalybeate and saline properties are

combined. Such a compound water as this is found at Chel-
tenham. Acidulous waters contain much free acid, usually
carbonic, which imparts to it a sparkling character. At times,
the acid is muriatic or sulphuric. Sulphureous water abounds
in sulphuretted hydrogen gas. It is often used medicinally,
and is extremely unpalatable. The waters of Harrowgate are
of this class.

The above tests will at once show the character of any proposed water, and by evaporating a quantity to dryness, and
weighing the solid residue, the quantity of earthy matter may
be arrived at. For the purpose of dissolving out, in hot
water, the properties of immersed substances, the softer the
water is the better; but when it is only to soften and but
slightly change the character of any substance, as, for instance,
in cooking vegetables, hard water is by some people supposed .
to be superior; it prevents their colouring matter and properties
from being abstracted. This may be owing either to the direct
chemical action of the salts, or to their occupying the spaces
between the pores of the liquid. Some water may be kept
with impunity in leaden vessels; with others the attempt is
highly dangerous. Acids act upon lead; but with sulphuric,
arsenic, hydrodic, and phosphoric, a crust is formed on the
surface of the metal, which thus protects the lead from
further action. Water charged, therefore, with these acids,
may safely be kept in lead; but if the acid be carbonic, the
result is very different; the crust is not a protecting one, but
mixes with the water as fast as it is formed, thus leaving a
clear surface of lead always ready to be acted upon, and
disseminating through the mass of water a poisonous salt of
lead.

It is important, however, to observe that whatever may be
the chemical qualities of the water obtained from a well, there
is always a great danger attending its use as a beverage, unless
there be a consumption sufficiently great to keep up a continually renewed supply. Necessarily in such positions the
water is, to a greater or less degree, stagnant; it can be but

E

little aerated, and from its lengthened contact with the earth, or the sides of the well, it must be exposed to take up any soluble salts they may contain, particularly the carbonates or the sulphates of lime, which are very likely to be furnished by the masonry. It is also known that town wells are affected to a serious extent by the nitrates arising from the decomposition of the organic matter which permeates the soil. Baron Liebig and Dr. A. Smith have respectively detected the presence of the nitrates in the wells both of Giessen and Manchester, and the same fact occurs in London to a surprising extent. The waters so affected are very unwholesome, of a disagreeable flavour, and likely to produce cholic.

In lining or steining wells, therefore, it is advisable to use only silicious materials, or bricks so thoroughly burnt as not to be able to part with the carbonate of lime originally contained in the earth of which they are made, and to bed these materials in Roman cement, or at least in a lime obtained from the calcination of a decidedly argillaceous limestone. Chalk lime, or the common grey lime used near London, should be rejected in all works of this description.

Great care should also be taken to isolate any well from the infiltrations of dung-pits, cesspools, cemeteries, dead wells, or other sources from which it might be exposed to receive any nitrates. As the infiltrations from these sources occasionally extend to considerable distances, great precautions are required to insure their perfect exclusion. But after all these precautions may have been taken, the sources of impurity are so numerous in large towns that it may fairly admit of question whether, as a matter affecting public health, it can ever be advisable to resort to shallow wells as a source of supply for domestic purposes in such positions. Of course this remark does not apply to the open country; but even there, the precautions above enumerated with respect to the construction and position of the wells must be observed.

APPENDIX.

THE description of the following Example is considered well worthy of remark, as it tends to show the great advantage arising from a plentiful supply of water, together with the ease with which it is often obtained in districts apparently wanting in that necessary article.

At Bulphan Fen, within a few miles of Aveley, Essex, is a large tract of grass-land, situated at a low level, and liable to be much flooded in the winter season. Its value was formerly little, as in the summer time it was destitute of good water, being wholly dependent upon the pools and ditches which retained the remains of the winter's rain and floods. This rendered it unfit for stock, as, in addition to the small quantity of water remaining, even that was rendered bad by the heat of the weather. The landowners in the neighbourhood were induced to bore, and, being successful in finding springs, the water from which overflowed the surface of the ground, their example was followed by the proprietor of the Artesian well under consideration, who, together with his father, suffered much inconvenience from the scarcity of water upon 300 acres of low grass-land at Aveley. A spot was fixed upon at the edge of the uplands, and about the level of high-water mark of the Thames: during the month of August, 1835, the work was commenced. The bore of the auger was 3 inches. The first 5 or 6 feet were an alluvial soil, mixed with many small stones, the whole of a gravelly nature ; succeeding this was a very soft, boggy ground, which ran in as fast as bored out ; into it were inserted wrought-iron pipes of the usual construction: the thickness of this bog was about 2 feet. The next substance was light brown sand, very close, firm, sharp, and fine ; it became darker as the work proceeded, till, at 65 feet from the surface, it was almost black. Separating this sand and the chalk, was a small portion of light, grass-green, flaky rock. In the chalk were layers of flints ; and the boring was carried on in this formation about 35 feet, when the auger and rods suddenly dropped seven feet into a cavity of very soft, almost liquid chalk, from which the water rose to within one foot of the surface of the marsh : water had been met with previously, but not in such large quantities as this spring furnished ; and, no doubt, the water from this would have risen higher but for its connection with other and weaker springs, which reduced its standing level by abstracting a portion of the water instead of adding thereto, notwithstanding the greater hydrostatic pressure exer-cised upon the lower and stronger spring: it must, therefore, always be borne in mind, that where a great rise of water is wished for from a deep strong spring, all others should be very carefully blocked out ; when quantity, and not standing level, is the question, the conditions of the case are altered. To return from this digression : the water in this well, which, as before remarked, rose almost to the surface, was conducted by a 2-inch pipe, inserted 3 inches under the water-level, into ditches traversing the land; the water ran white for some days, but ultimately perfectly clear, and continues to run night and day. The temperature is 51° Fahr. winter and summer, and the quantity delivered in 24 hours about 30,000 gallons ; it supplies 2 miles of ditches 10 feet wide, from which it runs into the sea.

In the neighbourhood of the above Artesian bore are situated some wells of the ordinary kind; the spring or springs to which they are sunk are strong, the water rising to the same level as in the Artesian one ; they receive their supply from the saturated sand spoken of above, and which is situated upon the top of the chalk. The identity of level between the wells is, no doubt, owing to their communication, which is established by the water from the chalk rising outside the pipe which lines the bore, the water naturally preferring such an exit to rising higher inside the pipe itself. Even with the most carefully executed work, it is difficult to prevent water rising outside the boring-pipes where they pass through sand; therefore, in ordinary cases, such an effect may be expected to take place, unless the lower springs are separated from the upper by an impermeable collar of clay or other matter through which the pipe passes.

Artesian Well at the New Model Prison.

The annexed description of the well at the New Model Prison is taken from an excellent notice published in the work entitled 'Papers of the Royal Engineers,' vol. vi., by Lieutenant-Colonel Jebb, under whose direction the work was executed. The following specification was submitted for competition to several well-sinkers, their estimate and tenders being founded on it:

Specification for sinking an Artesian Well at the Model Prison, Caledonian Road.

To sink a well, so as to be 6 feet diameter in the clear within the brickwork, to the depth of 150 feet. The price for each succeeding 30 feet complete to be stated. To be steined with 9-inch brickwork, with malm paviours, the back steining to have three courses in cement at every 5 feet, and the double, or inner steining, to have four courses in cement at every 10 feet.

The brickwork to be completed in successive portions of 5 feet, or less, if found necessary. The bricks to be of the best quality; the Roman cement to be mixed with one equal proportion of clean, sharp river-sand. Should it be found necessary to sink to a greater depth (not exceeding 30 feet), the contractor will state in his tender at what price per foot he will execute the same, in every respect as above specified.

To fix 9 feet of 12-inch cast-iron pipe at the bottom of the shaft, and to bore with a 10½-inch auger, and continue with the same down to the chalk, inserting in the bore cast-iron pipes 8 inches diameter, and not less than ⅝ths of an inch thick on the sides, fitted together with turned joints and wrought-iron collars, and fitted with screws; the whole to be flush inside and outside.

To continue boring in the chalk, with a 7½-inch auger, to such depth as will secure good water from the main spring, and in such quantity as may be considered necessary.

The whole of the above works are to be done in a workmanlike manner, with materials of the best description of their respective kinds, and to the entire satisfaction of the superintending officer.

The contractor will state at what price per foot, or per 10 feet, including the iron pipes, he will bore until he reaches the chalk; and at what price per foot, or per 10 feet, he will bore through the chalk until the necessary quantity of good water is obtained. Also at what price per foot he will provide and fix perforated copper pipes, 6½ inches diameter outside, weighing 6 ℔s. per foot, in the chalk, as far as may be necessary. The prices stated in the tender are to include every expense, the finding of all materials, scaffolding, tackle, cartage, &c., the stopping out the land-springs in an effectual manner, and every expense requisite for the entire completion of the work, excepting the removal of the earth excavated. If pumps are required during the execution of the work, they are to be supplied by the contractor, together with labour in pumping, and troughs for carrying off the water, without extra charge. Stone corbels, for supporting permanent framing, will be furnished to the contractor, to be inserted in the brickwork without extra charge.

The tender of Mr. Thomas Clark, of Tottenham, was considered as the most advantageous, and was, therefore, accepted. The tender was as follows:

Tender for sinking an Artesian Well at the Model
Prison. .

Tottenham.

I hereby tender to sink a shaft so as to be 6 feet diameter
in the clear within the brickwork, to the depth of 150 feet,
and to provide such materials as are required by the specification, and to perform the work in every way agreeably thereto ;
and to fix a 12-inch cast-iron pipe, 9 feet long, at the bottom
of the shaft, at the following prices :

			£.	s.	d.
1st 30 feet, for the sum of	67	10	0
2nd do. do.	57	0	0
3rd do. do.	58	10	0
4th do. do.	60	0	0
5th do. do.	61	10	0

Also to sink as many feet further as the superintending officer
may consider necessary, so as not to exceed 30 feet, for the
sum of £2. 5s. per foot ; also to bore to the chalk with a
10½-inch auger, and fix pipes of the diameter required, and
fitted together as specified, for the sum of £2. 2s. per foot ;
also, to bore in the chalk with a 7½-inch auger to such depth
as may be considered necessary by the superintending officer,
for the sum of £1. 7s. per foot ; and if it should be determined
to insert perforated copper pipes in the boring in the chalk,
I hereby tender to supply the same, to weigh not less than
6 lbs. to the foot, and to fix the same in the bore for the
further sum of 10s. 2d. per foot ; and in every other respect
to conform to the specification, and to complete the whole of
the work in a proper and workmanlike manner, and to the
satisfaction of the superintending officer.

   (Signed)   THOS. CLARK.

To Capt. JEBB, Royal Engineers.

In commencing the work five men were employed, who
made an excavation 9' 6" diameter, which was to allow space
for the finished shaft to be 6' 0" in the clear, with the 9-inch

steining, and 12 inches of puddle at the back, for more effectually excluding the land-springs. This excavation was carried down to the depth of 10 feet. The 9-inch steining in cement and the puddle were then commenced, and completed to the surface. The stratum of clay at this depth was so solid, that it was considered that the puddle might be dispensed with; an excavation only 7 feet 6 inches in diameter, and 5 feet deep, was therefore made, and the back steining only, of half a brick in thickness, completed in cement. Similar excavations of five feet in depth were made in succession, the back steining alone in each case being completed, until the solid mass of London blue clay was found, at the depth of 30 feet from the surface. The inner steining was then brought up in cement, so as to underpin the first portion which had been completed. The land-springs were found to be effectually excluded, and the work then proceeded in all respects according to the specification. Two additional hands were employed when the well was about 30 feet deep, and no difficulty was experienced until the mass of London clay was cut through, and the upper beds of the plastic clay formation, which were found at the depth of 150 feet, were perforated. Here a stratum of dark sand was found, containing a little water. This sand was so loose that it did not afford sufficient foundation for the brickwork; and there was this further difficulty, that had the water been pumped out, the sand would have been set in motion, or, to use a technical expression, would have blown up in the well. Under these circumstances, it was determined to substitute cast-iron cylinders, five feet diameter and one inch thick, for the brick steining.

The specification and tender for supplying the cylinders, and executing the work with them, was as follows:

Tender for supplying cast-iron cylinders to be used in lieu of steining.

Tottenham.

I hereby engage to secure the present brickwork in its

place by strong elm ribs, suspended by iron rods up the shaft, and to provide and fix cast-iron cylinders of five feet diameter and one inch thick, in five-feet lengths, with internal flanges, properly packed and bolted together, and to caulk the same with iron cement, and to carry them down through the upper sand, and drive the lower end firmly into the clay; and to concrete behind the upper cylinder with gravel and cement, to form a footing for the lower steining, and for stopping out water, providing every material required for the work, at £7. 2s. per foot lineal.

(Signed)   THOS. CLARK.

Before proceeding to lower the well or fix the cylinders, it was necessary to secure or tie up the brickwork which had been already executed. For this purpose a strong elm frame was inserted under it, and the frame being connected by 1¼-inch rods, with two strong beams fixed over the top of the well, effectually secured the steining in its place. In order to steady the cylinders, and keep them in a right line as the work proceeded, four battens, 20 feet long, 7 inches wide, and 2½ inches thick, were fixed to the lower part of the brickwork, forming a kind of frame through which the cylinders would slide; this being arranged, the first cylinder, five feet in length, was lowered to the bottom, and, after being properly adjusted by means of wedges, another was added on the top, and the joint of the flanges made good; four others were added in succession, making a length of 30 feet of cylinders fixed, before the excavation was proceeded with. The object of this was twofold; first, that the outer surface of the cylinders being confined within the wooden frame already described, the true direction would be maintained; and, secondly, that the weight of the mass would aid in its descending into its place as the boring or excavation was proceeded with: by these means, had the stratum proved to be a quicksand, the difficulty would have been overcome: a stage was then placed on the upper part of the cylinders, and

an auger, 4' 10" in diameter, was introduced within them.
Each time that this auger was drawn out, the cylinders
settled on an average about two inches, and no difficulty was
experienced. The stratum of sand, which was about 20 feet
in depth, was cut through, and a hard mottled clay was found
under it: it was essential that the cylinders should be firmly
fixed in the clay, in order to prevent the water contained in
the sand from forcing its way under them, and rising into the
well. The boring was therefore continued for a few feet,
and the cylinders were at last driven into the clay with a
heavy dolly, made of the rough trunk of a tree. The water,
which had hitherto stood above the level of the top of the
sand in the cylinders, was now pumped out, and the well ·
remaining perfectly dry, afforded evidence that the water contained in the sand had been effectually stopped out. The
12-inch pipe mentioned in the original specification was dispensed with, and the boring was continued with a 10½-inch
auger down to the chalk; 8-inch pipes were then introduced,
which were firmly fixed several feet into the chalk, and were
left standing six feet above the bottom of the cylinders. The
object of this latter arrangement was, that any sediment
contained in the water might settle at the bottom of the
well.

The following is a section of this well, together with the
distance from the surface of the ground to various points in
the well itself:

Yellow clay and gravel	30	0
Blue clay	100	0
Mottled clay	19	6
Dark loamy sand, and little water . . .	18	0
Hard mottled clay and sand, without water .	17	0
Dark sand, with little water	34	0
Hard flint	1	0
Chalk	151	0
Total depth	370	6

Distance of bottom of brick shaft to surface . 153 0
„ from top of iron cylinders to do. . 139 0
„ from bottom of iron cylinders to do. . 170 0
„ from bottom of iron piping to do. . 230 0
„ from top of copper piping to do. . 220 0
„ from bottom of copper piping to do. . 259 0

On the completion of this well, it was considered desirable to test the strength of the spring by pumping, which operation had also the effect of freeing the sides of the bore, thereby allowing the water to percolate more quickly, as the action of the tools necessarily had a tendency to harden the chalk. The pump was kept at work night and day; a relieving gang of men coming on every four hours. After working in this manner for 48 hours, the level of the water in the cylinders was marked, and it was also ascertained that in one hour rather more than 900 gallons were removed from the well. The water-level was lowered by the pumping one foot; and as a hole five feet in diameter and one foot deep contains 122 gallons (see page 55), that amount deducted from 900, gives as the water-supply nearly 800 gallons per hour.

THE END.

LONDON:
BRADBURY AND EVANS, PRINTERS, WHITEFRIARS.

A

CATALOGUE OF WORKS

IN

ARCHITECTURE (CIVIL AND NAVAL),

AGRICULTURE, CHEMISTRY, ELECTRICITY,

ENGINEERING (CIVIL, MILITARY, & MECHANICAL),

MATHEMATICS, MECHANICS, METALLURGY,

ETC. ETC.

AND

Books in General & School Literature.

INCLUDING

MR. WEALE'S

SERIES OF RUDIMENTARY WORKS,

SERIES OF EDUCATIONAL WORKS, AND

SERIES OF GREEK AND LATIN CLASSICS.

PUBLISHED BY

LOCKWOOD AND CO.

STATIONERS' HALL COURT, LONDON, E.C.

1859.

THE FAVOURITE FIRST FRENCH BOOK FOR A CHILD.

LA BAGATELLE:

Intended to introduce Children of five or six years old to some knowledge of the French Language. Revised by MADAME N. L. New and Cheaper Edition, much improved, and embellished with entirely new cuts. 18mo, price 2s. 6d., bound and lettered.

"Will be f and to answer its intended purpose in every respect; and the volume can certainly lay claim to the merit of being produced with more than an average amount of care, so far as its typographical getting-up is concerned."—*Illustrated Times.*

"A very nice book to be placed in the hands of

children; likely to command their attention by its beautiful embellishments."—*Papers for the Schoolmaster.*

"A well-known little book, revised, improved, and adorned with some very pretty new pictures. It is, indeed, French made very easy for very little children."—*The School and the Teacher.*

Twelfth Edition, 8vo, 432 pages, reduced from 10s. 6d. to 7s. 6d. cloth.

LE BRETHON'S FRENCH GRAMMAR:

A GUIDE TO THE FRENCH LANGUAGE.

By J. J. P. LE BRETHON. Revised and corrected by L. SANDIER, Professor of Languages.

"A thorough practical book."—*Critic.*
"Of the many works that have come under our notice for teaching French, this excels them all."—*Hants Advertiser.*
"The great merit of this Grammar undoubtedly

is its clearness and simplicity of arrangement."—*Sun.*
"Deserves universal acceptation as the plainest, easiest, and completest Grammar ever published."—*Educational Gazette.*

Seventh Edition, considerably improved, with new plates substituted, 4to, 5s., cloth,

VOCABULAIRE SYMBOLIQUE ANGLO-FRANCAIS;

Pour les Elèves de tout Âge et de tout Degré; dans lequel les Mots les plus utiles sont enseignés par des Illustrations. Par L. C. RAGONOT, Professeur de la Langue Française.

A SYMBOLIC FRENCH AND ENGLISH VOCABULARY.

For Students of every Age, in all Classes; in which the most Useful and Common Words are taught by Illustrations. By L. C. RAGONOT, Professor of the French Language. The Illustrations comprise, embodied in the text, accurate representations of upwards of 850 different objects, besides nine whole-page copper-plates, beautifully executed, each conveying, through the eye, a large amount of instruction in the French Language.

.*. This work in the Anglo-French form having been extensively adopted, not only in Great Britain and on the Continent, but also in America the publishers have determined to adapt it to other languages, and by producing it in a more portable form, to render it equally suitable to the Tourist and the General Scholar. The following is now ready,

8vo, 6s., red cloth, lettered,

SYMBOLISCHES ENGLISCH-DEUTSCHES WÖRTERBUCH:

THE

SYMBOLIC ANGLO-GERMAN VOCABULARY;

Adapted from the above work. Edited and Revised by FALCK LEBAHN, Ph. Dr., Author of "German in One Volume," "The German Self Instructor," &c. With 850 woodcuts, and eight full page lithographic plates.

THE CHEAPEST SCHOOL ALGEBRA.

Seventh Edition, 12mo, 300 pages, reduced to 3s. 6d., bound,

NICHOLSON AND ROWBOTHAM'S PRACTICAL SYSTEM OF ALGEBRA.

DESIGNED FOR THE USE OF SCHOOLS AND PRIVATE STUDENTS.

THE

HISTORICAL LINES OF DR. GREY'S TECHNICAL MEMORY.

With various additions, chiefly as they apply to modern history. Arranged for general use. Sixth Edition, 1s., sewed.

A

CATALOGUE OF WORKS

IN

ARCHITECTURE, AGRICULTURE,
CHEMISTRY, ENGINEERING, MATHEMATICS, MECHANICS,
METALLURGY, &c. &c.

PUBLISHED BY

LOCKWOOD & CO.,

STATIONERS' HALL COURT, E.C.

COMPLETE LIBRARY OF THE MILITARY SCIENCES.

*Three vols., royal 8vo, upwards of 500 Engravings and Woodcuts, in extra cloth boards,
and lettered, 4l. 10s.; or may be had in six separate parts, paper boards,*

AIDE-MÉMOIRE TO THE MILITARY SCIENCES.

Framed from Contributions of Officers of the different Services, and edited by a Committee of the Corps of Royal Engineers. The work is now completed.
*** This work is admirably adapted as a present to the young Military Student, and should find a place on the shelves of every Regimental Library. It is recommended to the notice of Volunteer Rifle or Artillery Corps.

ALBAN ON THE HIGH PRESSURE ENGINE.

In 8vo, with 29 fine plates, 16s. 6d. cloth,

THE HIGH PRESSURE STEAM ENGINE.

An Exposition of its Comparative Merits, and an Essay towards an Improved System of Construction, adapted especially to secure Safety and Economy.

By DR. ERNST ALBAN,
Practical Machine Maker, Plau, Mecklenburg.

TRANSLATED FROM THE GERMAN, WITH NOTES,

By WM. POLE, C.E., F.R.A.S., Assoc. Inst. C.E.

BUCK ON OBLIQUE BRIDGES.

Second Edition, imperial 8vo, price 12s. cloth,

A PRACTICAL AND THEORETICAL ESSAY ON OBLIQUE BRIDGES,

With 13 large Folding Plates.

By GEORGE WATSON BUCK, M. Inst. C.E.
Second Edition, corrected by W. H. BARLOW, M. Inst. C.E

A SYNOPSIS OF PRACTICAL PHILOSOPHY.

ALPHABETICALLY ARRANGED,

containing a great variety of Theorems, Formulæ, and Tables, from the most accurate and recent authorities, in various branches of Mathematics and Natural Philosophy : to which are subjoined small Tables of Logarithms. Designed as a Manual for Travellers, Architects, Surveyors, Engineers, Students, Naval Officers, and other Scientific Men.

By the Rev. JOHN CARR, M.A.,
Late Fellow of Trinity College, Cambridge.

₊ Sir John Macniel, C.E., a good authority, recommends this work to his pupils and friends.

THE CARPENTER'S NEW GUIDE;

Or, Book of Lines for Carpenters. Comprising all the Elementary Principles essential for acquiring a knowledge of Carpentry, founded on the late PETER NICHOLSON'S standard work.

A New Edition, revised by ARTHUR ASHPITEL, Arch., F.S.A. ;

TOGETHER WITH PRACTICAL RULES ON DRAWING,

By GEORGE PYNE, Artist.

THE PRACTICAL RAILWAY ENGINEER.

A Concise Description of the Engineering and Mechanical Operations and Structures which are combined in the Formation of Railways for Public Traffic ; embracing an Account of the Principal Works executed in the Construction of Railways to the Present Time ; with Facts, Figures, and Data, intended to assist the Civil Engineer in designing and executing the important Details required for those Great Public Works.

By G. DRYSDALE DEMPSEY, Civil Engineer.
Fourth Edition, revised and greatly extended.

With 71 double quarto plates, 72 woodcuts, and Portrait of GEORGE STEPHENSON.

LIST OF PLATES.

1 Cuttings	33 Creosoting, screw-piling, &c.	53 Watering apparatus—
2—4 Earthworks, excavating	34 Permanent way and rails	(A.) Tanks
5 Ditto, embanking	35 Ditto, chairs	54 Ditto, (B.) Details of pumps
6 Ditto, waggons	36 Ditto, fish-joints, &c.	55 Ditto, (C.) Details of engines
7 Drains under bridges	37 Ditto, fish-joint chairs	56 Ditto, (D.) Cranes
8 Brick and stone culverts	38—9 Ditto, cast-iron sleepers,&c.	57 Hoisting machinery
9 Paved crossings	40 Ditto, Stephenson's, Brunel's,	58 Ditto, details
10 Railway bridges, diagram	Heman's, Macneill's, and	59 Traversing platform
11—14 Bridges, brick and stone	Dnckray's	60 Ditto, details
15—16 Ditto, iron	41 Ditto, Crossings	61 Station-roof at King's Cross
17—21 Ditto, timber	42 Ditto, ditto, details	62 Ditto, Liverpool
22 Centres for bridges	43 Ditto, spring-crossings, &c.	63 Ditto, Birmingham
23—27 "Pont de Montlouis"	44 Ditto, turn-table	64—5 Railway Carriages
28 "Pont du Cher"	45—6 Terminal station	66 Ditto, details
29 Suspension bridge	47—49 Stations	67—8 Railway Trucks and wheels
30 Box-girder bridge	50 Goods stations	69 Iron and covered waggons
31 Trestle bridge and Chepstow	51 Polygonal engine-house	70 Details of brakes
bridge	52 Engine-house	71 Wheels and details
32 Details of Chepstow bridge		72 Portrait

BARLOW ON THE STRENGTH OF MATERIALS.

With Nine Illustrations, 8vo, 16s. cloth,

TREATISE ON THE STRENGTH OF TIMBER,

CAST IRON, MALLEABLE IRON,

And other Materials ; with Rules for Application in Architecture, the Construction of Suspension Bridges, Railways, &c. ; and an Appendix on the Powers of Locomotive Engines on horizontal planes and gradients.

By PETER BARLOW, F.R.S.,

Hon. Member Inst. Civil Engineers, &c.

A New Edition by J. F. HEATHER, M.A., of the Royal Military Academy, Woolwich.

WITH AN ESSAY ON THE EFFECTS PRODUCED BY CAUSING WEIGHTS TO TRAVEL OVER ELASTIC BARS.

By PROF. WILLIS, of Cambridge.

———◆———

GREGORY'S MATHEMATICS, BY LAW.

Third Edition, in 8vo, with 13 Plates, very neatly half-bound in morocco, 1l. 1s.

MATHEMATICS FOR PRACTICAL MEN.

Being a Common Place Book of Pure and Mixed Mathematics, designed chiefly for the use of Civil Engineers, Architects, and Surveyors.

By OLINTHUS GREGORY, LL.D., F.R.A.S.

Third Edition, revised and enlarged by HENRY LAW, Civil Engineer.

CONTENTS.

PART I.—PURE MATHEMATICS.
Chapter I. Arithmetic.—Chap. II. Algebra.—Chap. III. Geometry.—Chap. IV. Mensuration.—Chap. V. Trigonometry.—Chap. VI. Conic Sections.—Chap. VII. Properties of Curves.

PART II.—MIXED MATHEMATICS.
Chapter I. Mechanics in General.—Chap. II. Statics.—Chap. III. Dynamics.—Chap. IV. Hydrostatics.—Chap. V. Hydrodynamics.—Chap. VI. Pneumatics.—Chap VII. Mechanical agents.—Chap. VIII. Strength of Materials.—Appendix of Tables.

———◆———

A COMPLETE BODY OF HUSBANDRY, BY YOUATT.

Tenth Edition, much enlarged, with numerous Engravings, 8vo, price 12s. cloth, lettered, gilt back.

THE COMPLETE GRAZIER,

AND FARMER'S AND CATTLE BREEDER'S ASSISTANT.

A Compendium of Husbandry : containing full instructions on the breeding, rearing, general management, and medical treatment of every kind of stock, the management of the dairy, and the arrangement of the farm offices, &c.; description of the newest and best agricultural implements ; directions for the culture and management of grass land, and of the various natural and artificial grasses, draining, irrigation, warping, manures, &c.

By WILLIAM YOUATT, Esq., V.S.,

Member of the Royal Agri. Soc. of England; Author of "The Horse," "Cattle," &c.

THE GREAT EASTERN AND IRON SHIPS IN GENERAL.

Second Edition, Atlas of Plates, with separate text, price 1l. 5s.,

ON IRON SHIP-BUILDING.

With Practical Examples and Details, in Twenty-four Plates, including three of the *Great Eastern*, together with Text containing Descriptions, Explanations, and General Remarks, for the use of Ship-owners and Ship-builders.

By JOHN GRANTHAM, C.E.,
Consulting Engineer and Naval Architect, Liverpool.

*** A work on the construction and build of Ships, by the application of Iron, has become now of the utmost importance, not only to Naval Architects, but to Engineers and Ship-owners. The present Work has been prepared, and the subjects drawn, in elevation, plan, and detail, to a scale useful for immediate practice, in a folio size, with figured dimensions, and a small Volume of text (which may be had separately, price 2s. 6d.)

DESCRIPTION OF PLATES.

1 Hollow and bar keels, stern and stern posts.
2 Side frames, floorings, and bilge pieces.
3 Floorings continued—keelsons, deck beams, gunwales, and stringers.
4 Gunwales continued—lower decks, and orlop beams.
5 Angle-iron, T iron, Z iron, bulb iron, as rolled for iron ship-building.
6 Rivets, shown in section, natural size, flush and lapped joints, with single and double riveting.
7 Plating, three plans, bulkheads, and modes of securing them.
8 Iron masts, with longitudinal and transverse sections.
9 Sliding keel, water-ballast, moulding the frames in iron ship-building, levelling plates.
10 Longitudinal section, and half breadth deck plans of large vessels, on a reduced scale.
11 Midship sections of three vessels of different sizes.
12 *Large vessel,* showing details—*Fore-end* in section, and end view with stern posts, crutches, deck beams, &c.
13 *Large vessel,* showing details—*After-end* in sec-

tion, with end view, stern frame for screw, and rudder.
14 *Large vessel,* showing details—*Midship section,* half-breadth.
15 *Machines* for punching and shearing plates and angle-iron, and for bending plates; rivet hearth.
16 *Machines.*—Garforth's riveting machine, drilling and counter sinking machine.
17 *Air furnace* for heating plates and angle iron; various tools used in riveting and plating.
18 *Gunwale,* keel, and flooring; plan for sheathing iron ships with copper.
19 Illustrations of the magnetic condition of various iron ships.
20 Gray's floating compass and binnacle, with adjusting magnets.
21 Corroded iron bolt in frame of wooden ship; caulking joints of plates.
22 *Great Eastern.*—Longitudinal sections and breadth plans.
23 *Great Eastern.*—Midship section, with details.
24 *Great Eastern.*—Section in engine room, and paddle boxes.

READY RECKONER, INCLUDING FRACTIONAL PARTS OF A POUND WEIGHT.

24mo, 1s. 6d. cloth, or 2s. strongly bound in leather,

THE INSTANT RECKONER.

Showing the Value of any Quantity of Goods, including Fractional Parts of a Pound Weight, at any price from One Farthing to Twenty Shillings : with an Introduction, embracing copious Notes of Coins, Weights, Measures, and other Commercial and Useful Information ; and an Appendix, containing Tables of Interest, Salaries, Commission, &c.

SIMMS ON LEVELLING.

Fourth Edition, with 7 plates and numerous woodcuts, 8vo, 8s. 6d., cloth.

A TREATISE ON THE PRINCIPLES AND PRACTICE OF LEVELLING,

Showing its application to purposes of Railway and Civil Engineering, in the Construction of Roads, with Mr. TELFORD's Rules for the same.

By FREDERICK W. SIMMS, F.G.S., M. Inst. C.E.

Fourth Edition, with the addition of Mr. Law's Practical Examples for setting out Railway Curves, and Mr. Trantwine's Field Practice of Laying out Circular Curves.

THE LAND VALUER'S BEST ASSISTANT.

Being Tables, on a very much improved Plan, for Calculating the Value of Estates. To which are added, Tables for reducing Scotch, Irish, and Provincial Customary Acres to Statute Measure; also, Tables of Square Measure, and of the various Dimensions of an Acre in Perches and Yards, by which the Contents of any Plot of Ground may be ascertained without the expense of a regular Survey, Miscellaneous Information on English and Foreign Measures, Specific Gravities, &c.

By R. HUDSON, Civil Engineer.

"This new edition includes tables for ascertaining the value of leases for any term of years; and for showing how to lay out plots of ground of certain acres in farms, square, round, &c., with valuable rules for ascertaining the probable worth of standing timber in any amount; and is of incalculable value to the country gentleman and professional man."—*Farmer's Journal.*

TABLES FOR THE PURCHASING OF ESTATES,

Freehold, Copyhold, or Leasehold, Annuities, Advowsons, &c., and for the renewing of leases held under cathedral churches, colleges, or other corporate bodies, for terms of years certain, and for lives ; also, for valuing reversionary estates, deferred annuities, next presentations, &c., the Five Tables of compound interest, the Government Table of Annuities, and an extension of SMART's Tables.

By WILLIAM INWOOD, Architect.

The Seventeenth Edition, with considerable additions, and new and valuable Tables of Logarithms for the more difficult computations of the Interest of Money, Discount, Annuities, &c., by Mons. FEDOR THOMAN, of the Société Crédit Mobilier, Paris.

COMMERCIAL HANDBOOK OF CHEMICAL ANALYSIS;

Or, Practical Instructions for the Determination of the Intrinsic or Commercial Value of Substances used in Manufactures, in Trades, and in the Arts.

By A. NORMANDY,

Author of " Practical Introduction to Rose's Chemistry," and Editor of Rose's " Treatise of Chemical Analysis."

"We recommend this book to the careful perusal of every one; it may be truly affirmed to be of universal interest, and we strongly recommend it to our readers as a guide, alike indispensable to the housewife as to the pharmaceutical practitioner."—*Medical Times.*

"A truly practical work. To place the unscientific person in a position to detect that which might ruin him in character and fortune, the present work will prove highly valuable. No one can peruse this treatise without feeling a desire to acquire further and deeper knowledge of the enticing science of chemical analysis."—*Expositor.*

"The author has produced a volume of surpassing interest, in which he describes the character and properties of 400 different articles of commerce, the substances by which they are too frequently adulterated, and the means of their detection."—*Mining Journal.*

"The very best work on the subject the English press has yet produced."—*Mechanics' Magazine.*

NORMANDY'S CHEMICAL ATLAS AND DICTIONARIES.

*The Atlas, oblong folio, cloth limp, 1l. 1s., the Dictionaries, post 8vo, 7s. 6d., cloth ;
or, Atlas and Dictionaries together, 1l. 8s. cloth.*

THE CHEMICAL ATLAS;

Or, Tables, showing at a glance the Operations of Qualitative Analysis. With Practical Observations, and Copious Indices of Tests and Re-actions ; accompanied by a Dictionary of Simple and of Compound Substances, indicating the Tests by which they may be identified ; and a Dictionary of Re-agents, indicating their preparation for the Laboratory, the means of testing their purity, and their behaviour with Substances.

By A. NORMANDY,

Author of "The Commercial Handbook of Chemical Analysis," &c., &c., and Editor
of H. Rose's "Treatise of Chemical Analysis."

"Tables such as these, like Maps and Charts, are more eloquent than the clearest prose statement. It is the most elaborate and perfect work of the kind that we are acquainted with."—*Mechanics' Magazine.*

"The work gives evidence of the author being perfect master of the task he has undertaken, and will no doubt occupy a place in the library of every chemical student and analyst."—*Mining Journal.*

"Several works on chemical analysis have for many years held a high position in the estimation of the scientific chemist. The work before us will be found in our opinion far more useful to the student of analysis, nay more, to the practitioner. The directions are more minute, and the number of cases introduced infinitely more varied. There is scarcely a possible case which the author has not provided for. From a careful examination we are able to say that any person possessed of a slight

knowledge of chemical manipulation, may, by means of the Atlas and Dictionaries soon make himself a proficient analyst. Everyone who studies the Atlas must be impressed with the magnitude of the author's labour, and the vast extent to which he has economised the time and trouble of those who avail themselves of his friendly assistance."—*The Chemist.*

"'Normandy's Chemical Atlas' for comprehensiveness and completeness far surpasses anything of the kind hitherto published. I feel convinced that the student may with the aid of the Dictionaries, with which the Atlas is accompanied, successfully and alone undertake the examination of the most heterogeneous mixture, whether composed of organic or inorganic substances, or of both combined."—*Henry M. Noad, F.R.S., Lecturer on Chemistry at St. George's Hospital.*

By the same Author, crown 8vo, price 4s. 6d., cloth,

THE FARMER'S MANUAL OF AGRICULTURAL CHEMISTRY;

With Instructions respecting the Diseases of Cereals, and the Destruction of the Insects which are injurious to those plants. Illustrated by numerous woodcuts.

"This work will be found of incalculable value to the Farmer. We have perused it with much interest, and have no hesitation in recommending it to the notice of every farmer, who will find it an excellent guide in all questions of Agricultural Chemistry."—*Agricultural Magazine.*

"By far the best attempt to supply a treatise of a limited kind on the chemical analysis of the materials with which the agriculturist is concerned ; the instructions are very satisfactory, and are accompanied by illustrative figures of the necessary apparatus."—*Aberdeen Journal.*

————◆————

SPOONER ON SHEEP.

Second Edition. 12mo., 6s. cloth.

THE HISTORY, STRUCTURE, ECONOMY, AND DISEASES OF THE SHEEP.

In Three Parts. Illustrated with fine Engravings from Drawings by W. Harvey, Esq.

By W. C. SPOONER, V.S.,

Member of the Council of the Royal College of Veterinary Surgeons ; Honorary Associate of the Veterinary Medical Association ; Author of "Treatise on the Influenza," and the "Structure, Diseases, &c., of the Foot and Leg of the Horse ;" Editor of White's "Cattle Medicine," and White's "Compendium of the Veterinary Art."

"The name of Mr. Spooner, who is a distinguished member of his Profession, is a sufficient guarantee for the accuracy and usefulness of its contents. Farmers' clubs ought to add this work

to their libraries: and, as a work of reference, it ought to be in the possession of all Sheep Farmers."—*Gardeners' Chronicle.*

NOAD'S ELECTRICITY.

Fourth Edition, entirely re-written, in One Volume, illustrated by 500 woodcuts, 8vo, 1l. 4s. cloth,

A MANUAL OF ELECTRICITY.

Including Galvanism, Magnetism, Dia-magnetism, Electro-Dynamics, Magno-Electricity, and the Electric Telegraph.

By HENRY M. NOAD, Ph.D., F.C.S.,

Lecturer on Chemistry at St. George's Hospital.

Or in Two Parts :

Part I., ELECTRICITY and GALVANISM, 8vo, 16s. cloth.

Part II. MAGNETISM and the ELECTRIC TELEGRAPH, 8vo, 10s. 6d. cloth.

"This publication fully bears out its title of 'Manual.' It discusses in a satisfactory manner electricity, frictional and voltaic, thermo-electricity, and electro-physiology. To diffuse correct views of electrical science, to make known the laws by which this mysterious force is regulated, which is the intention of the author, is an important task."—*Athenæum.*

"Dr. Noad's Manual, in some departments of which he has had the counsel and assistance of Mr. Faraday, Sir William Snow Harris, Professor Tyndall, and others, giving an additional sanction and interest to his work, is more than ever worthy of being received with favour by students and men of science. The style in which it is written is very exact and clear."—*Literary Gazette.*

"Dr. Noad's 'Manual of Electricity' has for several years ranked as one of the best popular treatises on this subject. By an excellent method of arrangement, and a clear and agreeable style, he introduces the student to a sound elementary knowledge of every department of electrical science."—*Atlas.*

"This is a work of great merit, and is creditable to the scientific attainments and philosophical research of the author. Too much praise cannot be bestowed on the patient labour and unwearied application which were necessary to produce a work of such absorbing interest to the whole

trading and commercial community."—*Educational Gazette.*

"On the subject of electricity, it is a service second only to discovery, when one competent for the ask undertakes to sift and reconstruct the old materials, and to bring together and incorporate them with all that is important in the new. Such a service Dr. Noad has performed in his 'Manual of Electricity.'"—*Chambers' Journal*

"As a work of reference, this 'Manual' is particularly valuable, as the author has carefully recorded not only his *authorities*, but, when necessary, the *words* in which the writers have detailed their experiments and opinions."—*Mechanics' Magazine.*

"Among the numerous writers on the attractive and fascinating subject of electricity, the author of the present volume has occupied our best attention. It is worthy of a place in the library of every public institution, and we have no doubt will be deservedly patronised by the scientific community."—*Mining Journal.*

"The encomendations already bestowed in the pages of the *Lancet* on further editions of this work are more than ever merited by the present. The accounts given of electricity and galvanism are not only complete in a scientific sense, but, which is a rarer thing, are popular and interesting."—*Lancet.*

TREDGOLD ON THE STRENGTH OF IRON, &c.

Fourth Edition, in Two Vols., 8vo, 1l. 4s., boards (either Volume may be had separately),

A PRACTICAL ESSAY ON THE STRENGTH OF CAST IRON AND OTHER METALS ;

Intended for the assistance of Engineers, Iron-Masters, Millwrights, Architects, Founders, Smiths, and others engaged in the construction of machines, buildings, &c. ; containing Practical Rules, Tables, and examples founded on a series of new experiments ; with an extensive table of the properties of materials.

By THOMAS TREDGOLD, Mem. Inst. C.E.,

Author of "Elementary Principles of Carpentry," "History of the Steam Engine," &c. Illustrated by several engravings and woodcuts. Fourth Edition, much improved and enlarged. By EATON HODGKINSON, F.R.S.

HODGKINSON'S RESEARCHES ON IRON.

. Vol. II. of the above consists of EXPERIMENTAL RESEARCHES on the STRENGTH and OTHER PROPERTIES of CAST IRON : with the development of new principles ; calculations deduced from them ; and inquiries applicable to rigid and tenacious bodies generally. By EATON HODGKINSON, F.R.S. With Plates and Diagrams, 8vo, 12s. boards.

COTTAGES, VILLAS, AND COUNTRY HOUSES.

In 4to, 67 Plates, 1l. 1s. cloth,

DESIGNS AND EXAMPLES OF COTTAGES, VILLAS, AND COUNTRY HOUSES.

Being the Studies of Eminent Architects and Builders, consisting of plans, elevations, and perspective views; with approximate estimates of the cost of each.

RYDE'S TEXT BOOK FOR ARCHITECTS, ENGINEERS, SURVEYORS, &c.

In One large thick Vol. 8vo, with numerous engravings, 1l. 8s.

A GENERAL TEXT BOOK,

For the constant Use and Reference of Architects, Engineers, Surveyors, Solicitors, Auctioneers, Land Agents, and Stewards, in all their several and varied professional occupations; and for the assistance and guidance of country gentlemen and others engaged in the Transfer, Management, or Improvement of Landed Property, containing Theorems, Formulæ, Rules, and Tables in Geometry, Mensuration, and Trigonometry; Land Measuring, Surveying, and Levelling; Railway and Hydraulic Engineering; Timber Measuring; the Valuation of Artificers' Work, Estates, Leaseholds, Lifeholds, Annuities, Tillages, Farming Stock, and Tenant Right; the Assessment of Parishes, Railways, Gas and Water Works; the Law of Dilapidations and Nuisances, Appraisements and Auctions, Landlord and Tenant, Agreements, and Leases. Together with Examples of Villas and Country Houses.

By EDWARD RYDE, Civil Engineer and Land Surveyor,
Author of several Professional Works.

To which are added several Chapters on Agriculture and Landed Property,

By Professor DONALDSON,
Author of several Works on Agriculture.

CONTENTS.

WHEELER'S AUCTIONEERS', &c., ASSISTANT.

24mo, cloth boards, 2s. 6d.

THE APPRAISER, AUCTIONEER, AND HOUSE-AGENT'S POCKET ASSISTANT,

For the valuation, purchase, and the renewing of Leases, Annuities, Reversions, and of Property generally; prices for inventories, with a Guide to determine the value of the interiors, fittings, furniture, &c.

By JOHN WHEELER, Valuer.

TREDGOLD'S CARPENTRY. FOURTH EDITION.

In One large Vol. 4to., 2l. 2s., in extra cloth.

THE ELEMENTARY PRINCIPLES OF CARPENTRY ;

A Treatise on the pressure and equilibrium of timber framing, the resistance of timber, and the construction of floors, arches, bridges, roofs, uniting iron and stone with timber, &c., with practical rules and examples ; to which is added, an essay on the nature and properties of timber, including the method of seasoning, and the causes and prevention of decay, with descriptions of the kinds of wood used in building ; also numerous tables of the scantlings of timber for different purposes, the specific gravities of materials, &c.

By THOMAS TREDGOLD, Civil Engineer.

Illustrated by fifty-three Engravings, a portrait of the author, and several Woodcuts. Fourth Edition, corrected and considerably enlarged. With an Appendix, containing specimens of various ancient and modern roofs.

Edited by PETER BARLOW, F.R.S.

CONTENTS OF PLATES.

HANDY BOOK FOR ACTUARIES, BANKERS, INSURANCE OFFICES, AND COMMERCIAL MEN IN GENERAL.

In 12mo, cloth, price 5s.

THEORY OF COMPOUND INTEREST AND ANNUITIES,

With TABLES of LOGARITHMS for the more difficult computations of Interest, Discount, Annuities, &c., in all their applications and uses for Mercantile and State purposes, with a full and elaborate introduction.

By FEDOR THOMAN, of the Société Crédit Mobilier, Paris.

"A very powerful work, and the Author has a very remarkable command of his subject."—*Professor A. de Morgan.*

"No banker, merchant, tradesman, or man of business ought to be without Mr. Thoman's truly 'handy-book.'"—*Review.*

"The author of this 'handy-book' deserves our thanks for his successful attempt to extend the use of logarithms."—*Insurance Gazette.*

"We recommend it to the notice of actuaries and accountants."—*Athenæum.*

WEALE'S ENGINEER'S POCKET BOOK.

With 8 copper plates, and numerous woodcuts, in roan tuck, 6s.

THE ENGINEER'S, ARCHITECT'S, AND CONTRACTOR'S POCKET BOOK.

Published annually. With DIARY of EVENTS and DATA connected with Engineering, Architecture, and the kindred Sciences, professionally and otherwise revised.

CONTENTS FOR 1860.

Alloys. Almanack
Ballasting. Barlow
Barrel Drains
Bessemer on the Manufacture of Iron and Steel
Boilers and Engines (Proportions of)
Boilers, Furnaces, and Chimneys
Calendar
Carpentry and Joinery
Cask and Malt Gauging
Castings, sundry for Sewers, Gasworks, &c.
Cast-Iron Columns and Girders
Chairs for Railways
Chimneys, dimensions of
Circumference of Circles
Circular Area (Tables of)
Circle, Cylinder, Sphere, &c.
Coal Experiments; Economic Values of Coals
Coking (evaporative Powers of Coal, and Results of)
Columns, Posts, &c.
Copper Mines (Synopsis of) in Devon and Cornwall
Cornwall Pumping-Engines
Current Coins
Du Buat
Earthwork
East London Waterworks
Eclipses
Elastic Properties of Steam
Ellipses, Cones, Frustrums, &c.
Ephemerides of the Planets
Fairbairn on the Mechanical Properties of Metals; on the tensile strength of Wrought Iron at various temperatures; Tabular Girder Bridges; Notes on Toughened Cast-Iron: on the Resistance of Tubes to Collapse
Flooring
French and English Scales
Friction
Fuel on the American Railways and on English Railways
Gas Engineers' Calendar

Gauges (List of) and Weights of Galvanized Tinned Iron Sheets
Girders (Cast-Iron)
Hawksley
Heat (Effects of)
High Water at London Bridge
Howard
Hydraulics
Hydrodynamics
Institution of Civil Engineers (List of Members of)
Institute of British Architects (List of Members of)
Iron Bar
Iron
—— Roofs
Knot Tables
Latitudes and Longitudes [&c.
Log. of Sines, Cosines, Tangents, &c.
Marine Engines
Marine Screw Propulsion
Marsilier
Masonry
Mensuration (Epitome of)
Morin's Experiments on Friction; on Ropes
Natural Sines, &c.
Neville, on Measuring Walls
Notes to accompany the Abbreviated Table of Natural Sines
Peninsular and Oriental Steam Fleet
Prokin [and Boilers
Proportions of Marine Engines
Proportional Sizes and Weights of Hexagon-heads and Nails for Bolts
Pumping Water by Steam Power Rails
Rennie (G.); Messrs. Rennie
Roofs
Ropes, Experiments of
Sewers
Sleepers for Railways
Smith's Sewer. Sound
Specific Gravity of Gases
Square, Rectangle, Cube, &c.
Square and Round Bar-Iron

Strength of Columns
Strength of Materials of Construction
Strength of Rolled T-Iron
Stone, Preservation of
Stones
Tables of the Weight of Iron Castings for Timber Roofs
—— of the Properties of Different Kinds of Timber
—— of the Weights of Rails and Chairs
—— of the Weight, Pressure, &c. of Materials, Cast-Iron, &c.
—— of Weights of Copper, Tin-Plates, Copper-Pipes, Locks for Coppers, Leaden Pipes
—— for the Diameters of a Wheel of a Given Pitch
—— of the Weights of a Lineal Foot of Flat Bar-Iron, of a Superficial Foot of Various Metals, &c.
—— of the Weight of a Lineal Foot of Cast-Iron Pipes
—— of the Diameter of Solid or Cylinder of Cast-Iron, &c.
—— of the Diameter and Thickness of Metal of Hollow Columns of Cast-Iron
—— of Cast-Iron Stanchions
—— of Strength of Cast-Iron Bars
—— of the Values of Earthwork
—— of Weights and Measures
—— of Natural Sines
Teeth of Wheels
Telford's Memorandum Book
Thermometers
Timber for Carpentry and Joinery
Tredgold's Rails
Waterworks
Weights of Copper, Brass, Steel, Hoop-Iron, &c.
Weights and Measures
Weights of Rails
Wickstead
Woods

MR. WEALE'S SERIES OF RUDIMENTARY, SCIENTIFIC, EDUCATIONAL, AND CLASSICAL WORKS,

At prices varying from 1s. to 2s. 6d.

Lists may be had on application to MESSRS. LOCKWOOD & CO.

⁎⁎⁎ This excellent and extraordinarily cheap series of books, now comprising upwards of 150 different works, in almost every department of Science, Art, and Education, is strongly recommended to the notice of Mechanics' Institutions, Literary and Scientific Associations, Free Libraries, Colleges, Schools and Students generally, and also to Merchants, Shippers, &c.

CATALOGUE

OF

RUDIMENTARY, SCIENTIFIC, EDUCATIONAL, AND CLASSICAL WORKS

FOR

COLLEGES, HIGH AND ORDINARY SCHOOLS, AND SELF-INSTRUCTION.

ALSO FOR

MECHANICS' INSTITUTIONS, FREE LIBRARIES, &o., &o.

MR. WEALE'S

SERIES OF RUDIMENTARY WORKS

FOR THE USE OF BEGINNERS.

LONDON: JOHN WEALE, 59, HIGH HOLBORN.

WHOLESALE AGENTS, LOCKWOOD & CO., 7, STATIONERS' HALL COURT, E.C.

The several Series are amply illustrated, in demy 12mo., each neatly bound in cloth; and, for the convenience of purchasers, the subjects are published separately at the following prices:

1. CHEMISTRY, by Prof. Fownes, F.R.S., including Agricultural Chemistry, for the use of Farmers . . . . 1s.
2. NATURAL PHILOSOPHY, by Charles Tomlinson 1s
3. GEOLOGY, by Major-Gen. Portlock, F.R.S., &c. . . . . 1s. 6d.
4, 5. MINERALOGY, with Mr. Dana's additions, 2 vols. in 1 . . . 2s.
6. MECHANICS, by Charles Tomlinson . . . . 1s.
7. ELECTRICITY, by Sir William Snow Harris, F.R.S. . . . 1s. 6d.
7.* ON GALVANISM; ANIMAL AND VOLTAIC ELECTRICITY; Treatise on the General Principles of Galvanic Science, by Sir W. Snow Harris, F.R.S. 1s. 6d.
8, 9, 10. MAGNETISM, Concise Exposition of, by the same, 3 vols. in 1. 3s. 6d.
11, 11* ELECTRIC TELEGRAPH, History of the, by E. Highton, C.E. . . 2s.
12. PNEUMATICS, by Charles Tomlinson . . . . 1s.
13, 14, 15, 15.* CIVIL ENGINEERING, by Henry Law, C.E., 3 vols.; and Supplement by G. R. Burnell, C. E., in 1 vol. . . . 4s. 6d.

124. On Roofs for Public and Private Buildings, founded on Dr. Robinson's Work . . . . 1s. 6d.

124*. Recently constructed Iron Roofs, Atlas of plates . . 4s. 6d.

125. On the Combustion of Coal and the Prevention of Smoke, Chemically and Practically Considered, by Chas. Wye Williams, M.I.C.E. . . . . { The 2 vols. } 3s.
126. Illustrations to ditto . . . . { in 1. }

127. Rudimentary and Practical Instructions in the Art of Architectural Modelling, with illustrations for the Practical Application of the Art, by J. A. Richardson, Arch. . . . 1s. 6d.

128. The Ten Books of M. Vitruvius on Civil, Military, and Naval Architecture,* translated by Joseph Gwilt, Arch., 2 vols. in 1, *in the press* . . . . 2s. 6d.

129. Atlas of Illustrative Plates to ditto, in 4to, with the Vignettes, designed by Joseph Gandy, *in the press* . . . . 4s. 6d.

130. Introduction to the Study and the Beauty of Grecian Architecture, by the Right Hon. the Earl of Aberdeen, &c., &c., &c., *in the press* . . . . 1s.

MR. WEALE'S
NEW SERIES OF EDUCATIONAL WORKS.

1, 2, 3, 4. Constitutional History of England, by W. D Hamilton . 4s.

5, 6. Outlines of the History of Greece, by the same, 2 vols. . 2s. 6d.

7, 8. Outline of the History of Rome, by the same, 2 vols. . 2s. 6d.

9, 10. Chronology of Civil and Ecclesiastical History, Literature, Art, and Civilisation, from the earliest period to the present, 2 vols. . . . . 2s. 6d.

11. Grammar of the English Language, by Hyde Clarke, D.C.L. . 1s.

11*. Hand Book of Comparative Philology, by the same . . 1s.

12, 13. Dictionary of the English Language. A new Dictionary of the English Tongue, as spoken and written, above 100,000 words, or 50,000 more than in any existing work, by the same, 3 vols. in 1 . . . . 3s. 6d.

14. Grammar of the Greek Language, by H. C. Hamilton . . 1s.

15, 16. Dictionary of the Greek and English Languages, by H. R. Hamilton, 2 vols. in 1 . . . . 2s.

17, 18. ——————— English and Greek Languages, by the same, 2 vols. in 1 . . . . 2s.

19. Grammar of the Latin Language, by the Rev. T. Goodwin, A.B. . 1s.

20, 21. Dictionary of the Latin and English Languages, by the same. Vol. I. . . . . 2s.

22, 23. ——————— English and Latin Languages, by the same. Vol. II. . . . . 1s. 6d.

24. Grammar of the French Language . . . . . . 1s.

* This work, translated by a scholar and an architect, was originally published at 36s. It bears the highest reputation, and being now for the first time issued in this Series, the student and the scholar will receive it as a boon from the gifted translator.

25. DICTIONARY OF THE FRENCH AND ENGLISH LANGUAGES, by A. Elwes.
  Vol. I. . . . . 1s.
26. ———————— ENGLISH AND FRENCH LANGUAGES, by the same.
  Vol. II. . . . . 1s. 6d.
27. GRAMMAR OF THE ITALIAN LANGUAGE, by the same . . . . 1s.
28, 29. DICTIONARY OF THE ITALIAN, ENGLISH, AND FRENCH LANGUAGES,
  by the same. Vol. I. . . . . 2s.
30, 31. ———————— ENGLISH, ITALIAN, AND FRENCH LANGUAGES,
  by the same. Vol. II. . . . . 2s.
32, 33. ———————— FRENCH, ITALIAN, AND ENGLISH LANGUAGES,
  by the same. Vol. III. . . . . 2s.
34. GRAMMAR OF THE SPANISH LANGUAGE, by the same . . . 1s.
35, 36, 37. 38. DICTIONARY OF THE SPANISH AND ENGLISH LANGUAGES,
  by the same, 4 vols. in 1 . . . . 4s.
39. GRAMMAR OF THE GERMAN LANGUAGE . . . . . 1s.
40. CLASSICAL GERMAN READER, from the best authors . . . 1s.
41, 42, 43. DICTIONARIES OF THE ENGLISH, GERMAN, AND FRENCH LAN-
  GUAGES, by N. E. Hamilton, 3 vols., separately 1s. each . 3s.
44, 45. DICTIONARY OF THE HEBREW AND ENGLISH LANGUAGES, containing the Biblical and Rabbinical words, 2 vols (together with the
  Grammar, which may be had separately for 1s.) by Dr. Bresslau,
  Hebrew Professor . . . . 7s.
46. ———————— ENGLISH AND HEBREW LANGUAGES. Vol. III.
  to complete . . . . 3s.
47. FRENCH AND ENGLISH PHRASE BOOK . . . . . . 1s.

THE SERIES OF EDUCATIONAL WORKS

*Are on sale in two kinds of binding; the one for use in Colleges and Schools
and the other for the Library.*

HAMILTON'S OUTLINES OF THE HISTORY OF ENGLAND, 4 vols. in 1. strongly
  bound in cloth . . . . 5s.
————————Ditto, in half-morocco, gilt, marbled edges . . . 5s. 6d.
HISTORY OF GREECE, 2 vols. in 1, bound in cloth . . . 3s. 6d.
Ditto, in half-morocco, gilt, marbled edges . . . . 4s.
HISTORY OF ROME, 2 vols. in 1, bound in cloth . . . . 3s. 6d.
Ditto, in half-morocco, gilt, marbled edges . . . . 4s.
CHRONOLOGY OF CIVIL AND ECCLESIASTICAL HISTORY, LITERATURE, ART,
  &c , 2 vols. in 1, bound in cloth . . . . . . 3s. 6d.
————————Ditto, in half-morocco, gilt, and marbled edges . . . 4s.
CLARKE'S DICTIONARY OF THE ENGLISH LANGUAGE, bound in cloth . 4s. 6d.
————————, in half-morocco, gilt, marbled edges . . . . 5s.
————————, bound with Dr. CLARKE'S ENGLISH GRAMMAR, in cloth . 5s. 6d.
————————Ditto, in half-morocco, gilt, marbled edges . . . 6s.

HAMILTON'S GREEK AND ENGLISH and ENGLISH AND GREEK DICTIONARY, 4 vols. in 1, bound in cloth . . . . 5*s.*

————Ditto, in half-morocco, gilt, marbled edges . . . 5*s.* 6*d.*

————Ditto, with the GREEK GRAMMAR, bound in cloth . . 6*s.*

————Ditto, with Ditto, in half-morocco, gilt, marbled edges . 6*s.* 6*d.*

GOODWIN'S LATIN AND ENGLISH and ENGLISH AND LATIN DICTIONARY, 2 vols. in 1, bound in cloth . . . . 4*s.* 6*d.*

———— Ditto, in half-morocco, gilt, marbled edges . . . . . 5*s.*

———— Ditto, with the LATIN GRAMMAR, bound in cloth . . 5*s.* 6*d.*

———— Ditto, with Ditto, in half-morocco, gilt, marbled edges . . 6*s*

ELWES'S FRENCH AND ENGLISH and ENGLISH AND FRENCH DICTIONARY, 2 vols. in 1, in cloth . . . . 3*s.* 6*d.*

———— Ditto, in half-morocco, gilt, marbled edges . . . . . 4*s.*

———— Ditto, with the FRENCH GRAMMAR, bound in cloth . . 4*s.* 6*d.*

———— Ditto, with Ditto, in half-morocco, gilt, marbled edges . . . 5*s.*

FRENCH AND ENGLISH PHRASE BOOK, or Vocabulary of all Conversational Words, bound, to carry in the pocket . . . . . 1*s* 6*d.*

ELWES'S ITALIAN, ENGLISH, AND FRENCH,—ENGLISH, ITALIAN, AND FRENCH,—FRENCH, ITALIAN, AND ENGLISH DICTIONARY, 3 vols. in 1, bound in cloth . . . . 7*s.* 6*d.*

ELWES'S Ditto, in half-morocco, gilt, marbled edges . . . . 8*s* 6*d.*

———— Ditto, with the GRAMMAR, bound in cloth . . . . 8*s.* 6*d.*

———— Ditto, with Ditto, in half-morocco, gilt, marbled edges . . 9*s.*

———— SPANISH AND ENGLISH and ENGLISH AND SPANISH DICTIONARY, 4 vols. in 1, bound in cloth . . . . 5*s.*

———— Ditto, in half-morocco, gilt, marbled edges . . . . 5*s.* 6*d.*

———— Ditto, with the GRAMMAR, bound in cloth . . . . . 6*s.*

———— Ditto, with Ditto, in half morocco, gilt, marbled edges . 6*s.* 6*d.*

HAMILTON'S ENGLISH, GERMAN, AND FRENCH,—GERMAN, FRENCH, AND ENGLISH,—FRENCH, GERMAN, AND ENGLISH DICTIONARY, 3 vols. in 1, bound in cloth . . . . 4*s.*

———— Ditto, in half-morocco, gilt, marbled edges . . . 4*s.* 6*d.*

———— Ditto, with the GRAMMAR, bound in cloth . . . . . 5*s.*

———— Ditto, with Ditto, in half-morocco, gilt, marbled edges . 5*s.* 6*d.*

BRESSLAU'S HEBREW AND ENGLISH DICTIONARY, with the GRAMMAR, 3 vols. bound in cloth . . . . 12*s.*

———— Ditto, 3 vols., in half-morocco, gilt, marbled edges . . . 14*s.*

Now in the course of Publication,

GREEK AND LATIN CLASSICS,

Price 1*s.* per Volume, (except in some instances, and those are 1*s.* 6*d.* or 2*s.* each), very neatly printed on good paper.

A Series of Volumes containing the principal Greek and Latin Authors, accompanied by Explanatory Notes in English, principally selected from the best and most recent German Commentators, and comprising all those

Works that are essential for the Scholar and the Pupil, and applicable for the Universities of Oxford, Cambridge, Edinburgh, Glasgow, Aberdeen, and Dublin,—the Colleges at Belfast, Cork, Galway, Winchester, and Eton, and the great Schools at Harrow, Rugby, &c.—also for Private Tuition and Instruction, and for the Library.

Those that are not priced are in the Press.

LATIN SERIES.

1 A new LATIN DELECTUS, Extracts from Classical Authors, with Vocabularies and Explanatory Notes . . . . . . *1s.*

2 CÆSAR'S COMMENTARIES on the GALLIC WAR; with Grammatical and Explanatory Notes in English, and a Geographical Index *2s.*

3 CORNELIUS NEPOS; with English Notes, &c. . . . . *1s.*

4 VIRGIL. The Georgics, Bucolics, and doubtful Works: with English Notes . . . . *1s.*

5 VIRGIL'S ÆNEID (on the same plan as the preceding) . . . *2s.*

6 HORACE. Odes and Epodes; with English Notes, and Analysis and explanation of the metres . . *1s.*

7 HORACE. Satires and Epistles, with English Notes, &c . . *1s. 6d.*

8 SALLUST. Conspiracy of Catiline, Jugurthine War . . . *1s. 6d.*

9 TERENCE. Andria and Heantontimorumenos . . . *1s. 6d.*

10 TERENCE Phormio, Adelphi and Hecyra . . . . *1s. 6d.*

11 CICERO. Orations against Catiline, for Sulla, for Archias, and for the Manilian Law.

12 CICERO. First and Second Philippics; Orations for Milo, for Marcellus, &c.

13 CICERO. De Officiis

14 CICERO. De Amicitia, de Senectute, and Brutus . . *1s. 6d.*

15 JUVENAL and PERSIUS. (The indelicate passages expunged).

16 LIVY. Books i to v. in 2 parts . *3s.*

17 LIVY. Books xxi. and xxii. . *1s.*

18 TACITUS. Agricola; Germania; and Annals, Book i.

19 Selections from TIBULLUS, OVID, PROPERTIUS, and LUCRETIUS.

20 Selections from SUETONIUS and the later Latin Writers . . *1s. 6d.*

GREEK SERIES,

ON A SIMILAR PLAN TO THE LATIN SERIES.

1 INTRODUCTORY GREEK READER. On the same plan as the Latin Reader . . . . . *1s.*

2 XENOPHON. Anabasis, i. ii. iii. . *1s.*

3 XENOPHON Anabasis, iv. v. vi. vii. . . . . . *1s.*

4 LUCIAN. Select Dialogues . . *1s.*

5 HOMER. Iliad, i. to vi . *1s. 6d.*

6 HOMER. Iliad, vii to xii . *1s. 6d.*

7 HOMER. Iliad, xiii. to xviii. *1s. 6d.*

8 HOMER. Iliad, xix. to xxiv. *1s. 6d.*

9 HOMER. Odyssey, i. to vi. *1s. 6d.*

10 HOMER. Odyssey, vii to xii. *1s. 6d.*

11 HOMER. Odyssey, xiii. to xviii.

12 HOMER. Odyssey, xix. to xxiv.; and Hymns

13 PLATO. Apology, Crito, and Phædo.

14 HERODOTUS, i. ii.

15 HERODOTUS, iii. to iv.

16 HERODOTUS, v. vi and part of vii.

17 HERODOTUS. Remainder of vii. viii. and ix.

18 SOPHOCLES; Œdipus Rex. . *1s.*

19 SOPHOCLES; Œdipus Colonæus.

20 SOPHOCLES; Antigone.

21 SOPHOCLES; Ajax.

22 SOPHOCLES; Philoctetes.

23 EURIPIDES; Hecuba.

24 EURIPIDES; Medea.

25 EURIPIDES; Hippolytus.

26 EURIPIDES; Alcestis.

27 EURIPIDES; Orestes.

28 EURIPIDES. Extracts from the remaining plays.

29 SOPHOCLES. Extracts from the remaining plays.

30 ÆSCHYLUS. Prometheus Vinctus.

31 ÆSCHYLUS. Persæ.

32 ÆSCHYLUS. Septem contra Thebas.

33 ÆSCHYLUS. Chœphoræ.

34 ÆSCHYLUS. Eumenides.

35 ÆSCHYLUS. Agamemnon.

36 ÆSCHYLUS. Supplices.

37 PLUTARCH. Select Lives.

38 ARISTOPHANES. Clouds.

39 ARISTOPHANES. Frogs.

40 ARISTOPHANES. Selections from the remaining Comedies.

41 THUCYDIDES, i. . . . . *1s.*

42 THUCYDIDES, ii.

43 THEOCRITUS, Select Idyls.

44 PINDAR.

45 ISOCRATES.

46 HESIOD.

LONDON : JOHN WEALE, 59, HIGH HOLBORN.

WHOLESALE AGENTS, LOCKWOOD & CO., 7, STATIONERS' HALL COURT, E.C.